GANG WAR

MATTHEW LEDREW

GANG WAR

CORAL BEACH CASEFILES

Published in Canada by Engen Books, St. John's, NL.

A CIP catalogue record for this book is available from Library and Archives Canada.
ISBN: 978-1-989473-26-9
Copyright © 2019 Matthew LeDrew

This book is a work of fiction. Names, characters, places and incidents are products of the author's imagination or are used fictitiously. Any resemblance to actual events or locales or persons living or dead is entirely coincidental.

Distributed by:
Engen Books
www.engenbooks.com
submissions@engenbooks.com

First mass market paperback printing: April 2012
Second mass market paperback printing: October 2019

Cover Image: Kit Sora Photography
Cover Design: Matthew LeDrew

For
Ellen

PROLOGUE

Tommy Irons held the knife firmly in his right hand with the blade pressed tight against his left wrist.

The knife belonged to his father. It was a simple hunting knife, its rubber handle wrapped in black grip tape. The faded six-inch blade came up sharp on both sides, without any serrated edges or designs in the metal to make it appear fancy or frightening.

Against his tender, loose flesh, it looked much more impressive than when it rested casually on his father's worktable.

His hair was spiked high, as it usually was, belaying its long length. His heart-shaped face, usually seen with a smile (or at least a grin), was now sewn up in a frown of deep resentment. He wore a stained and tattered white tee shirt under an open blue one. The shirt was denim, like his jeans. He'd fallen in love with that style three years ago after staying up late and watching old teen movies from the nineties and had gone shopping the next weekend. He owned at least a dozen identical pairs.

He sat on the edge of his bed, arms leaned against knees and feet thrown over the side. There were pictures scattered all around of the most recent person to leave him with nothing: Julie Peterson.

His walls were covered in images as well. Pictures that he had taken, pictures that had been taken of him and of his life.

That had always been an annual ritual of Tommy's. Every year, he'd change all of the pictures on his wall to those he'd taken the year before. His father had always called him Shutterbug for it, back when he'd given Tommy's actions any thought.

This year, however, had been different.

This year everyone had started to abandon him, from the beginning of the school semester starting with Jamie Dawkins and continuing through to Julie Peterson. The weeks could almost be marked by a personal loss on his part, either through death or choice or circumstance.

Every time one of them left him, he would turn their picture around. He would never take it down completely, merely flip it so that it faced the wall, sticking a pin in its corners and trying his best to forget the faces contained within them.

Now they were all facing front again. They glared at him again. Judged him again. The eyes that had once seemed warm and inviting now scowled and belittled him.

Jamie, forever frozen, held his cue stick as he awaited Mike to finish his turn. Half cut off by the table, his face was also lost but this time in the shadows of his red Cougars baseball cap. In the darkness, his eyes sparkled from the flash, looking sinister as they stared out at Tommy no matter where he sat in the room.

There were sunspots in Sara's picture, but they worked so well that they enhanced the image. Tommy had zoomed in on her face as she was sipping from the straw of what he thought might have been a Cherry Coke, although the can wasn't visible in the photo. He had framed the shot around her flawless face, accented with wisps of her blonde hair puffing out in stringy wet spikes from each of her black hair bands. Her eyes were wide, showing almost all of her pupils. The girl just didn't seem to believe in blinking, as he used to tell her after examining a roll of film in his darkroom. Now those eyes gawked at him, as if daring him into a staring contest he had no hope of winning even if she wasn't merely an image on glossy photo paper. It was so condescending, the way her eyes seemed to give him the once over, then push any thought of him aside, choosing death over him.

Then there was Derek.

There was no imagination needed to vilify that photo. Staring directly into the lens, arms crossed, eyes squinted and one eyebrow cocked -- he looked ready to leap from the photo and cut Tommy's head off, which he no doubt would have done if given half the chance. Then there was that grin. The sly smile prickling at the sides of his face, the one that he'd always worn. He wore it every day at school, while everyone around him talked about the murders, wondering who would be next and who could do such a thing. He smiled and joked and made light of it every single day... knowing all along that it was him. That he could have stopped and put their fears to rest at any time, but didn't. It was all to impress his father, who spent more time at his job than with his own son. The smile, those eyes... they made you feel like you were being stalked. Like it was only a matter of time, even through the camera's lens.

Then there was Julian Grendel, one of his best friends growing up, sitting back against the couch in his rumpus room, arms stretched out around Cathy and Liz as the both of them leaned in and pretended to give him a kiss on either cheek. His smile was broad. His big blue eyes clearly visible, their color brought out by the sea-green tee shirt he was wearing. He was mocking Tommy, holding out his hands around all that he had and Tommy did not. He was laughing at him, egging him on and yelling at him to do it -- to slice the flesh and let it bleed all over him.

Then there was Randy Owchar, hanging out at The Factory with Justin Langley and Sven Douglas. Never aware that Tommy was taking their picture, they were just loitering by the counter. One of them (Sven, maybe) was holding a Pepsi. As it turned out, all three of them had been Tees, a gang of idealistic thugs that thought way too much of town pride and formed by Randy's mentally disturbed father. Randy had betrayed and hurt them all in many ways, but none more than Tommy.

In the photo each Tee, but especially Randy, was turned away from him. If anything, it was more natural that -- like always -- they didn't give him a second thought. From his place on the bed, Tommy glared up at Randy's face, turned away and sneering at the former friend.

In the background of Randy's picture was Roxanne,

the waitress at The Factory. She, at least, was looking directly at the camera. A small grin stretched across her gorgeous face, which was framed by the few scattered wisps of her curly red hair, otherwise drawn up in a bow. She was bringing Randy a Coke, for which he was already reaching into his pocket for change. She, at least, had always been kind to him. She was also one of the women killed by Derek Smith, who explained to a reporter that his reason was to throw the authorities off his trail by killing people outside his circle. Ever since she died, The Factory had not been the same. Joan, the owner, hadn't had any spirit since that day. None of it was fun anymore, instead just a grim reminder of what it had once been, when they had at least been able to cling to the illusion that everything was normal and that they were all friends, despite their differences.

Tommy turned and closed his eyes tightly, batting away a few droplets of tears as he turned to the next picture. His grip relaxed around the knife, then tightened again. He sighed, opened his eyes, and looked straight at the photo of Frederick Windser, who most people just called Sud. The picture was a bust of him, his bald head gleaming under the flourescent lights of the school. He had a fist connecting with the palm of his hand in front of him, wrinkling his dark green sweater at the elbows, distorting the triangles that adorned its chest. He had a vivid, fake grimace on his face as he posed, but the truth of the matter was in his eyes. His eyes sparkled with the mischievousness and playfulness of his true spirit as he posed for his friend's picture. In those eyes were all of the many years of friendship that he had given to Tommy...

and the question of why Tommy had betrayed him. It stung more than any photo yet. The night before Sud's death, Tommy had been with his killer. Randy murdered him simply because of his hometown – dead because of a few measly miles -- and the artificial importance of the tags 'Tee' and 'Omega.'

And then there was Mandy.

Amanda Peterson, the light that shone on all their lives, bringing hope to all it touched. She had come to them in their darkest hour, when it seemed like there was no good left in this world, and gave them a glimpse of something better. Her flame burned strong, even as darkness threatened, and maintained her cheerfulness, zest for life and ability to forgive those who had wronged her.

This was part of the reason that Tommy had loved her so much.

In the end it had taken a beating, both physical and spiritual, to finally break her body... but not her spirit. Raped, beaten, tortured, mocked, spat upon... the hope was still in her face, even long after she was dead.

Now, from its perch on his wall, that glow bathed down on him from her pictures on his wall... a mockery of what it had been, for no picture could ever do it justice.

The first was of Cathy, Julie, and Mandy at the Factory. It was one of those spur-of-the-moment pictures that he had taken only because he had his camera on him at the time and they had not noticed that he was standing there until it was too late.

Those were the ones that he liked best. Not the ones where everyone stood in a line like they were getting their driver's licence photo, looking stone-loaded out of their minds with red eyes and pasty expressions or had fake smiles plastered over an otherwise dreary expression.

No, he preferred the pictures that were natural. When he could look and remember what people were like, not when they were all dressed up, but every-day normal, in case he ever forgot.

The three of them were sitting on one of the park benches that The Factory owners had bought from the city and fixed up, with an old fashioned street lamp hanging overhead. Where they'd gotten that piece of nostalgia, he'd never know. Never ask, either.

In the picture, Cathy was sipping on her bottle of Cherry Coke via a straw, her head turned slightly. The angle made her hair drape down over a good portion of her face, dividing it into angular lines. She was wearing a tank top with red and black vertical stripes. One of the shoulder straps had fallen over her shoulder, turning the picture from something simple into something sensual.

Julie had actually managed to see him right before he pressed the shutter. She'd been looking past him, at Xander. There was a quirky smirk on her face. When developing the photos and finding he had captured it, Tommy got so happy that he pinned it up while it was still wet, permanently staining the bedspread beneath it with photochemical dots.

And Mandy. She was doing something with her hair. She had both hands up, fixing her pigtails, inadvertently presenting her breasts through the sweater that she almost always wore, or at least some variation of it. There was nothing sexual about the pose, though. It was like

Gang War

looking at a portrait, a painting of a beautiful woman. If done right, there was nothing sexual about the nudity, just beauty. That was the way this was. It was simply her being her, as no other person could, with mouth open to say something to Julie, who was completely oblivious to Mandy's presence.

Tommy had loved that picture for that exact reason. The fact that there she was, being perfect, and nobody was paying attention to her.

Nobody else could see her glow.

Sighing, he turned from the wall to the bed and floor surrounding him.

There were thirty or more photos sprawled out on the floor. Some upside down, some overlapping the others, and none of them in any particular order. There were close shots, wide shots, medium shots, group shots, portrait shots, and the one semi-nude she'd let him do that time they got drunk in Grendel's cabin with Sara. All the shots, no matter their composition, had one thing in common:

They were all of Julie Peterson.

In some she was looking at him, others she was interacting with others. But in all of them, she had cute freckles across the bridge of her nose. She had effervescent green eyes that formed the basis by which every other color in the photos were judged. She had perfectly white teeth, just a little crooked in the front and always in a smile. She had a heart shaped face. She had brown hair with natural light streaks.

In all the photos, she was who she was: never posed and never fake.

One in particular had Julie sitting with Mandy on a bench just outside of school. He told Mandy under false pretenses that he was taking the picture solely of her, so she was posed perfectly, pretending to be a kind of funny-sexy. Julie had been turned toward the smoking section, saying something to Xander when he had called out her name, just before pressing the shutter release button. What resulted was the most natural shot of her possible, from the back wearing a slinky tank top, her head turned over her shoulder to look at him.

He also lingered at the semi-nude shot, in which her shirt was off, revealing a black bra underneath. Nobody in attendance had remembered him taking that picture, including Tommy himself. When he discovered it he had told no one, not even Sud.

Turning away from the pictures, he let a single tear dribble down his cheek as he pressed the knife in; slowly increasing pressure, hissing air as he drew blood, which gradually streamed down his arm.

Pursing his lips, he continued to push, driving deeper into the tender flesh. The pain was overwhelming, shooting in violent bursts between wrist and brain, then everywhere in-between.

Biting his lower lip as the pain got even worse, he held his breath, trying to summon the strength to push down just a little deeper...

His lungs fought back and Tommy heaved a great sigh. He relaxed his grip on the blade and let it fall to the bed. He stood. Cursing softly to himself, he looked around the room at all of the faces staring back at him again.

Sud

Mandy
Julie
Xander
Sud
Randy
Mandy
Cathy
Xander
Sara
Julie

"Argh!" he screamed, eyes bloodshot from pain and rage. He picked up the knife again and sliced it across the wall. Several pictures tore in half, some just below the neckline. Bellowing again, he sliced at the picture of Sud again and again, ripping it up with each strike until it was barely recognizable. He then turned the blade on Sara, and Jamie, and Derek, and Grendel, and Roxanne, and Mandy, and Julie. He tore them all to shreds, sending tiny pieces of photo-paper confetti fluttering in all directions as he waved his arms about wildly with the blade.

He sliced a photo of Xander directly in two vertically, splitting him into halves. He turned to the part of the wall that mainly portrayed Cathy and Mike, grabbing at them with hungry fingers and ripping through the glossy finish on the paper as though it were nothing.

Finally he stopped and looked at what he had done. Sweat poured down his brow and blood down his arm. His breath came in heavy, great gasps.

One photo remained on the wall, hanging from a single tack.

It was the shot of Randy, Sven and Justin, all hanging out at The Factory, awaiting their drinks. Slowly, he reached out with the tip of the blade, gently slicing away Sven and Justin and sending their pieces falling to the floor.

Stepping back and turning away for just a moment, he spun back around quickly and threw the knife as hard as he could at the picture. The knife burrowed a whole two inches into the wall, splitting Randy directly between the eyes.

Tommy stood there, breathing deeply as he squinted at the knife and waited for it to stop vibrating.

CHAPTER ONE
SHOCK

She threw the vase as hard as she could, without aiming it at anything in particular, just heaving it with as much force behind it as she could muster.

It burst against the wall just to the side of Lee Piercey. He had to duck just to avoid the shards of pottery and soil coming back at him.

"Jaylen!" he cried, his face livid with anger as he stood up again, brushing the dirt off of his shoulder. "What the hell is the matter with you?"

"Me?!" she screamed, pointing her finger at herself to bring the point home. "Excuse me, you son of a bitch. I found the goddamn letters!"

Lee's face went white.

She reached into the kitchen drawer behind her, pulled out a bound wad of envelopes and heaved them at him. They connected with his forehead, knocking him back a pace. The elastic band binding them snapped, sending letters fluttering about everywhere, spinning to the ground all around him like fake plastic flakes in a snowglobe.

Lee fumed as he watched them fall around him. He turned back to face his wife, finger extended, and a fiery red color now very apparent on his face.

"Well, maybe if you were doing your fucking job, I wouldn't have to go sneaking around like a goddamn child!"

"Me?" she laughed, pointing at her own chest. "I couldn't get it up if I *wanted* to, you impotent fuck! What the fuck does this one got that I don't? Testicles?"

"You shut the hell up," he barked, taking several menacing steps toward her, his jaw set.

"Get out!" she screamed, stepping back against the wall, fear flashing in her eyes.

He realized what she thought he was going to do, shaking his head spitefully. "You'd like that, wouldn't you?" he drawled.

"Leave," she repeated, standing up straight again.

Smiling and calming down, he nodded and turned back toward the hallway.

Lee entered the bedroom, slamming the door behind him. He knelt down and reached under the bed quickly, pulling out a leather suitcase and opening it. It was already full of clothes, razors, and a few other toiletries. He looked it over quickly, then zipped it up, slung it over his shoulder and headed back out the door.

He walked to the front door of the house, slipping off his loafers as he went. When he reached the porch, he pulled on his shoes and grabbed the keys to his car off the rack. He looked down at them, smiling. Slowly, he removed the house key and the mail key off of them. He held them in the palm of his hand, feeling their weight.

"Jaylen!" he called out to the kitchen, a smug look on his face.

There was no response.

He frowned, turning toward the room and tilting his head to try and see in. "Jaylen?"

Again, no answer.

Sighing, Lee walked across the carpet, tracking mud over it as he did. He turned to look at it, worried at first, then smiled. "Jaylen, I'm leaving the fucking keys on the kitchen table!" he yelled out, wondering where she had gone on such short notice.

He turned the corner to enter the kitchen and saw her, lying on the floor with a long red line drawn across her gut. Blood leaked out of her mouth and her glassy eyes looked into the distance.

"Jesus!" he screamed, dropping his keys and the suitcase to the floor.

He felt a sharp pain in his back and fell to the ground. He hissed, then looked at the rapidly pooling blood on the floor next to his face until his eyes finally closed and he drifted off to sleep.

ↂↂ

Xander Drew stared forward, entranced, at the row of lockers spread out before him. They were painted in the school's colors, an alternating pattern of red and orange.

His brown hair looked almost black, only accented by his attire: a tight-fitting black tee-shirt, leather jacket, and dark blue jeans. Even his eyes, usually a dark blue, looked exceptionally black.

His brow furrowed, scrunching his bushy eyebrows

as he stared at the sight before him, letting out a sorrow-
ful sigh.

One of the lockers, an orange one, was left hanging
open.

There were squares on the inside that were not as faded as the rest of the painted metal, where photographs
and a schedule had once been taped down. On the front
of the locker were paper swatches in the shapes of flowers
where stickers had been ripped off in a hurry, along with
the unmistakable sight of eraser-burn where something
had been scrawled in pencil and hastily eradicated.

Slowly, he brought a hand up to the fragmented bits
of paper stuck and traced one finger along the edges of the
once shining flower, feeling its coarse edges against his
skin. Again, he let out a long breath of air, which was almost visible as it reacted with the metal in the cool school
hallway.

His hand relaxed and clapped against his side as it
fell limply. His eyes continued to trace out every detail
of the door, trying to remember what each shape and
line had once been.

Quietly, respectfully, a figure came up beside him.
Then another, on the opposing side.

Cathy Kennessy held her schoolbooks tightly against
her chest, hiding the majority of her red tank top under
both them and the black wool sweater that was draped
around her shoulders and arms. Her raven hair fell down
flat on either side of her face, hiding it in effect, except for
one eye, her nose, and part of her lip. Blowing at a strand
to get it out of her way, she quickly pushed both lengths
back behind her ears, revealing a pale round face that no-

body would ever want hidden. Her feet shuffled beneath her loose-fitting blue jeans and heels as she followed his gaze to its target.

Opposite her, Mike Harris frowned and folded his taut arms as he saw the sight in front of him, shaking his head and making his blonde hair shimmy out of place. His shirt read 'SE MAG D NIM' across it, which his mother had had specially made for him a few years ago. It read 'MIND GAMES' when switched around, something he had once found mildly amusing. He watched Xander for a minute, waiting for his friend to address him. When he did not, he shot his girlfriend a look.

She crunched her brow at him, moving her head from side to side ever so slightly. Sighing in defeat, he turned toward the locker as well, looking at the faded decals and removed decor.

Finally Xander moved again, opening the door the rest of the way until it clicked against the locker next to it. Inside, almost hidden by the shadows, was a small white square of paper. Hand trembling, he reached in and carefully picked it up by the edges. He turned it over, even though he already knew what it was.

It was a picture of him, taken two months ago at one of those four-photos-for-a-dollar booths. He had a goofy smile on his face but it was the only one that Julie had of him.

"She's really gone," he said simply, the despair in his voice palpable as he gently slid the photo into his pocket, resuming his glare into the empty void of her shadowed locker.

"Yeah," Cathy breathed sympathetically. She placed

a hand on his shoulder and began rubbing it gently. "She really is."

He turned toward the floor, looking as though he might start to cry, then sucked it back with one long sniff and changing his look to something between anger, sadness, and resolve. "I really didn't think she'd actually go, y'know?" he smirked, turning from Cathy to Mike as he fought his eyes from tearing up, acknowledging their presence for the first time.

"None of us did," Mike agreed, looking at the locker now as if using it as an excuse not to make eye contact with Xander. "But I guess she had her mind made up."

Xander nodded. He sucked both his lips in, then plopped them back out. "Good," he said finally, forcing a smile. "Hopefully she'll be happy in Coral Cove, right?"

"Yeah," Cathy chirped.

"That's where Mandy was," he said. He could feel the ridges that the picture made in the fabric of his jeans. "That's where she belongs right now."

They both just nodded, realizing that no matter what they said he would continue talking until he was done.

"It's not like she's needed here," he chuckled forcibly. "It's not like I needed her or anything. We'll be fine without her. Just fine."

There was a long silence, and each of them turned back toward the locker, oblivious to the looks of their fellow students, who formed their own opinions on the trio's actions as they walked past.

Mike let out several long breaths, the last of which he segued into a tune.

Xander turned to look at him. Then Cathy followed

suit.

After a moment, he began to mouth words, then say them softly, not quite singing. "... hear them talk about it, on the radio..."

Cathy rolled her eyes and then hid behind her hand, peeking out from between her fingers.

"... did you try to read the writing, on the wall..."

Xander allowed a real, true grin to twitch at the corners of his mouth that grew slowly into a smile.

"... did you hear the voices say, 'I've heard it all before?'"

"It's like deja vu, all over again..." Mike finished, turning his head on an angle and laughing.

"Exactly what made you do that?" Cathy asked, taking down her hand once she was sure that the both of them were done.

Mike shrugged. "The suspense was killing me."

"Yeah. It beat me to it," Xander groaned, placing a palm against the front of the locker door and shutting it tight with a loud clang of metal on metal.

"Hardy har har," Mike said, in his best snot-nosed voice. "You're so funny I forgot to puke on Cathy's heels."

"Heels?" Xander smirked, raising an eyebrow as he turned toward her and noticing how much taller she looked compared to usual. "When did that happen?"

Cathy squinted, as Mike's eyes bugged out and he made a motion as if to duck and cover. "Two months ago," she said icily, squeezing her lips together.

"Eee," Xander squealed softly with a voice suddenly emasculated. He gritted his teeth and turned to the side.

"I knew that."

"Of course you did."

"I did."

"I believe you."

"No you don't."

"You're right," she agreed finally, again pushing a strand of her hair back, which promptly fell back to where it had been. "I'm a horrible liar. I admit that now."

Xander smiled, an event that faded as he turned back toward the metal rectangle he hadn't even been aware they were walking away from, even though they were across the hall from it now. "I just don't know what I'm going to do without her."

"Did you tell her?" Mike asked, leaning against the wall with his arms folded, examining the locker to see what magnetic hold it had over his friend.

"Tell her what?" he posed, unsure.

"That you don't know what you're going to do without her?"

Xander's face was expressionless, devoid of all but physical features, as he spoke. "No. I couldn't. If I had, she might have stayed."

Cathy smiled, reaching up and bringing his chin up until she was looking into his eyes. "But, on the other hand, if you'd told her, she might have stayed."

"She made her choice," he said. "I wasn't about to say anything to her to influence it or make her regret it once it was done... it wouldn't be fair."

"Because people in this town *always* play fair, don't they?" Mike drawled.

Cathy shot him a look.

"What?" Mike asked, spreading his arms as if to illustrate his point. "All I'm saying is, how fair is it that Jules had to make this decision without knowing the whole score? It's like playing Texas hold 'em when everyone else is playing straight. She only got to see half her cards before she decided to fold."

Xander pushed his fingers through his hair, making his forehead look twice as big in the process.

"Is it just me... or did that make a little sense?" Cathy asked quizzically, giving her lover a look.

"I always make sense. You guys just don't listen," Mike said smartly.

"None of it matters now," Xander said finally, swiping both hands across the air quickly. "Julie's gone, and I'm here, and why she left or why she didn't stay is irrelevant."

"Maybe she was pregnant," came a voice from behind them, almost so low that they couldn't hear.

Xander's eyes went wide, followed in suit by Mike and Cathy, as all three turned to see Tommy close his locker door and then lean against it. He was facing them, his patented smirk plastered across his face.

Xander took a step forward, his fists clenching without him even realizing it, as he glared at the taller man. His eyes burned with rage. "What... did you say?"

Tommy tried to contain his laughter and failed miserably, the chuckle erupting from his lips like a volcano. "I said someone probably knocked 'er up. Geez, you'd think you'd be in a better mood about it, unless it wasn't yours. First action you'd've gotten that wasn't off a dead chick, right?"

Xander drew back so quickly that the slowly gathering group of students didn't even see his motion, only the result. Tommy spun around quickly, his mouth distorted, blood spitting out onto the locker doors.

He slammed against the floor then immediately started to laugh again. He wiped the blood on his lips away with one sleeve as Xander glared down at him, fists still readied.

Mike came up behind Xander fast, pulling him back and shoving him against the far wall.

Xander tried only once to push away, but a quick look from Cathy ended the struggle.

"Oh, I get it," Tommy nodded, slowly rising to his feet as he tasted a sliver of the blood that was on his thumb. "You're going back to pretending you're not making googly eyes at Cathy, while she pretends not to make googly eyes at you?" he laughed. "Careful Xander, you might end up with another one pregnant... she's good at that."

Cathy turned to face the wall, trying to hide the tears that were welling up in her eyes.

Xander lunged again, something deep inside of him surging, wanting to rip into Tommy. He felt his claws aching within his fingertips, pulling at the skin until they were ready to burst. He let out a low growl deep within his throat, not loud enough for anyone but himself to hear.

Mike stopped him again, placing his palm flat against his friend's chest and shoving. "No," he said, turning from Xander back to Tommy, removing his hand. "He's not worth it."

Unnoticed by all, Cathy stiffened a little, her back straightening to ramrod precision.

Tommy snorted, looking to have too much laughter in him to express in one lifetime. "Oh, I'm so hurt. Whatever shall I fucking do? I'm not worth it. Oh no!"

Mike stepped forward, though not in a threatening way. "Y'know, as much of a jerk as he could be, I'm still glad Sud isn't around to see you acting like this."

Tommy met his gaze and clicked his tongue against the roof of his mouth. That stupid smile of his was still plastered across his face.

"You know what? Me too," he said cheerily, walking away from the three of them before turning left, stopping and deciding to go right instead.

Principal Shnieder watched the scene through the shutters of the glass door to his office as Tommy walked away from Mike and Xander, leaving them to console Cathy. He sighed, letting the plastic strips flip back into place as he held the phone tighter to his ear, laying the base back down on his desk.

"So, you see where I'm coming from," he said warmly. "These kids, they're starting to get out of control again. We can't have that. They need someone they can talk to, before another one decides to go crazy again... yes...yes."

While the person on the other end spoke, he carefully moved the letter opener on the corner of his desk and then adjusted the angle at which his business cards were facing.

"I know..." he said once they were done, nodding even though the person couldn't appreciate the gesture. "... I understand that it isn't the best of conditions for you.

No offense, but it isn't for us either. You're my last resort. I need you, Robert. More importantly, these kids need you, and..."

Principal Shnieder stopped in response. Smiling as he went back to his chair, he sat down and put his feet up on the desk before rubbing one hand back through his scalp. "I understand... this will not effect your other responsibilities... we will work around your schedule... tomorrow? Thank you."

He hung up the phone, a sly grin spread across his lips as he leaned back into his chair.

There was a courtesy knock at the door before a pretty brunette popped her head in. "You busy, Mr. Shnieder?" she asked politely. He noticed there was a blonde girl behind her, waiting patiently to see the Principal.

"Not at all, Jennifer," he said, sitting up straight and straightening the papers on his desk.

ᐊᐅ

Xander leaned against the ripped and torn pool table, lining up a shot at the yellow one ball. He strained his eyes to see it properly and then adjusted his focus to look past it so that he could glare at Tommy.

Tommy sat at the bar, sipping on his cola. He watched as a young waitress passed by him, taking notice of all of her assets, and gave her a quick wink.

Xander tightened his brow and attempted his shot. The one missed its intended mark of the corner pocket completely, instead clacking against the eight and sending them both against the wall. He sighed before getting up again, shooting another sidelong glare at Tommy and shaking his head.

Cathy got up, rubbed some chalk against the top of her stick and then laid the half-used cube of blue powder on the side of the table. She jolted up next to Xander, her hair bobbing against his shoulder. "You missed," she said simply, giving him a curt smile.

He acknowledged her (barely) with a short grunt, wringing his stick with both hands as he imagined walking over to Tommy and using it to beat that smug look off of his lips.

Off to one side, leaning against a corner, Mike smiled at the two of them. He took a bite out of his Skor bar, its crisp almost-too-sweet goodness snapping off in his mouth. He peered at Tommy too, but his gaze was mostly fixated on Cathy. She'd been through a lot the past few months, and he was glad that what Tommy had said had not hurt her any more than that moment. "Keep your chin up, Xander," Mike said, his mouth full of candy. "She always chokes on the third-last ball." As both contestants ignored him, Mike's eyes began to stray around the room. It had been a long time since they had all come here, the three of them, like this. From the looks of things, it had been a long time since anyone had.

There were mock Persian rugs for sale, pinned up against the far wall. Each of them was brightly colored with earth tones, all with completely different patterns but the exact same aroma. Though one he could never quite name, it was in every Asian market or authentic restaurant he had ever visited. Mike loved that smell, it reminded him of his one and only trip to Los Angeles when he'd bought a Japanese dub on Highlander for three dollars at a cart in one such market. It had been two disks for an 190-minute movie, something he had marveled at at the time, but now seemed quite mundane. He had been impelled to choose Highlander from the large pile of DVDs because every other title had been pornos where the preview on the back had been a garbled mix of English and Spanish.

Near the rugs was the arcade section: a special, sunken part of the Factory that constantly radiated swirling lights and different noises and taunts. As a child, it was like a Siren's call. Eventually, the noises faded into the background but every now and then, if one got too close, one would still be pulled in. Most likely to one of the one-on-one fighting games that dominated the area.

Close to that was the bar, kitchen and tables. That was where Mike's senses really kicked into overdrive, making him forget exactly why anyone would not want to come here. Besides the smell of cheap booze and cigarette smoke (a vile combination that wafted not from the patrons but from the kitchen staff), there was the distinct fragrance of burgers frying on a grill. Big, thick, meaty burgers so greasy that you could feel your arteries clog as they slid slowly down your throat. The first time he had ordered one, it had taken him nearly an hour to devour the entire thing. Even then, he had to throw out almost half of it while his friends weren't looking and telling them he had finished the rest in one bite. To this day, this was still considered an impressive feat and was brought up on occasion.

On the wall that was directly in front of him -- the one behind Xander and Cathy as she sank her high ball then moved in for another -- were movie posters lined up with sticky tack, covering the bad plastering like cheap wall-paper. There were about thirty in all, from Timecop and The Breakfast Club all the way up to X-Men, but as far as Mike was concerned there was only one. One that caught his attention the second his eyes fell anywhere near it and any time: the poster for American Beauty.

The one with the blonde girl laying in a bed of roses, looking up at you with that come hither look in her eyes, mouth partially open and hair spread out in a halo around her head. She looked sublimely innocent lying there with dark red rose petals covering her breasts and mid-section, tongue barely visible, as if another petal rest inside her mouth.

As Mike stared deeper and deeper into the poster, he began to wonder if her tongue was like a rose petal. Soft and tender and quick, with such an odd and sweet taste that one would spend the first moments of the kiss trying to pin it down before relinquishing that thought into her body. When the imaginary kiss broke off, it was no longer the girl from the movie laying on the bed, but Cathy.

Cathy lay there, twisting about and moving her legs from side to side, shaking the rose petals that covered her but never moving them entirely. The result was like a quart of alcohol on Mike's system, blurring his vision to anything else. His mouth went dry and he felt his legs buckle.

She brought her finger up to her lip and touched it briefly with her tongue, smiling devilishly. She giggled at him when he quivered, then glanced down at herself, as if only just realizing how titillating she actually was. Grinning just a little, she stood up. All the rose petals fell to the bed, except for a few that stayed in her raven hair. She walked toward him slowly, her supple breasts waiting to be caressed, as were the curves of her soft, smooth body. He could already imagine what she felt like. *Remember* what she felt like. He remembered the hot, the moist... but mostly, he remembered the distinct taste of lime on his lips when he had kissed her...

"Mike," Cathy said again, a little louder this time, bringing him out of his trance. "What were you thinking about?" she grinned, just like she had in his daydream. The similarity startled him at first, making him wonder if her clothes would now fall to the floor and she would walk toward him with that look in her eyes.

He cleared his throat, and took one final look back at the image on the wall. It had gone back to being the young girl from the movie. Still hot, but nowhere near as satisfying as where his mind had taken it. He turned back to Cathy, smiling genuinely. "Nothing, sweety," he said as she pulled him into a kiss, her rose petal darting in and out of his mouth.

Xander watched their lips move for a second, then turned away and scanned the room. There were a few girls sitting closer to the kitchen then they were, each of them about the age that Mandy had been, thirteen or fourteen. Tommy was looking at them, too, and for a moment both men realized that they were thinking the same thing.

Their eyes met from across the room, both steely and cold. There was a silent dare between each, a promise that no matter what happened this would not be over easily. It was like two countries declaring war after years of uneasy peace.

Finally grinning, Tommy got up and walked over to the two girls. They laughed a little at something that he said, then he sat down next to them.

Again Xander felt his hands wringing the neck of his stick, his teeth grinding together. "I really hate that guy," he said under his breath, turning away before he broke the cue in half. "Smug, stupid bastard. I should drag him outside right now and give him what's been coming to him for months. Since Grendel's party. Since that time he kept hitting on Mandy. Since..."

"Since he saved your girlfriend's life and then she got all chummy with him alone in her hospital room," Mike said, breaking off the kiss long enough to breathe the words, then going in for one more peck before the couple turned to face Xander.

"Yes," Xander said, pointing at him in weird agreement. "Exactly. That's..." he shook his head and walked closer to the two of them, his footfalls heavy. "You can't tell me you guys don't see what's happening here?"

Cathy frowned. She reached out and touched Xander's arm, then remembered what Tommy had said about the both of them and let it fall to her side. "He's just... he's going through something too right now. Maybe he's just not handling it as well."

Xander groaned before he leaned over the pool table and fired at the seven ball. It connected, but ricocheted off the eight and sent it into the side pocket. Xander's head sunk down between his arms as Cathy giggled, then held her hand over her mouth to hide it. He sighed, throwing a sidelong glance at her, then fired the rest of the balls into the pockets one by one. When that was done, he reached into his pants pocket and withdrew a plastic cigarette case, from which he grabbed a Camel then pressed it between his lips firmly.

"Must you?" Cathy tisked in disgust, curling her upper lip at the sight of it.

"I really must," he replied, flicking the flint on the Bic lighter until flame spouted out the top of it. He lit the tip of the smoke, then closed his eyes and took a long drag, a smirk spreading over his lips.

"Maybe Tommy isn't the only one handling this the wrong way," Mike sighed, watching his friend inhale.

"Give it a rest, already," Xander barked back, smoke puffing out of his nose and mouth.

Cathy recognized the way he exhaled. There was a different way for every emotion he was feeling, she discovered. The quick, short burst of smoke from both his nostrils and his mouth meant that he was hurting, typically. "Look, Xander, Julie's leaving was hard on all of us."

"You hated her," he returned, almost laughing.

"I did," she nodded, in the exact same, sympathetic tone of voice. "I really, really did. But you didn't. You..."

"Don't even say it, Cathy," Xander ordered, pointing two fingers at her, his smoke lodged between them. "Don't even think it."

"You loved her," she said, making his arm drop.

His other hand rose, massaging the bridge of his nose and covering his eyes.

Mike looked away, realizing that he probably wouldn't be a part of this conversation.

She stepped toward him and tried to get his hand away from his face so that she could look at him, but he refused. Frowning, she tried again. This time he relented and immediately threw both arms around her, placing his head on her shoulder (a feat much easier now that she wore heels).

Mike turned away from the two as Cathy cooed soothingly, feeling his chest start to heave as he tried to force it not to. He looked over at Tommy, who was chatting away with the two young girls. At that moment, he looked up and glared at Cathy and Xander, smiling briefly at Mike.

From behind Tommy, the door to the kitchen opened and Joan stepped out with a tray full of nachos and laid them down onto the bar.

Joan was a big woman, and she reminded most of the Factory's patrons of Roseanne Barr with her witty, sarcastic nature. Up until a few months ago she would have come out of that kitchen with a wide smile on her face, laughing at something one of the kids had done or stopping to tell a quick joke. But since Roxanne's death there were dark circles around her eyes all the time. There were no more jokes or laughs, only the grim reality that things weren't as they were supposed to be.

Maybe things wouldn't have been quite so bad if business hadn't taken such a horrible turn after all of the murders. It didn't matter that Derek Smith was behind bars, and would remain there for what he had done. The streets weren't considered safe anymore, and neither was The Factory.

Mike watched her cross the room, keeping his eyes anywhere except for Xander and Cathy, trying to give his friend as much space as possible. The last thing he needed right now was to feel crowded or boxed in by the two of them coming in at him.

Xander's cigarette hung loosely on his bottom lip. The smoke drew up into his eyes and made them sting harshly. He put up with the discomfort as the smoke served a more devious purpose: it kept Cathy from getting too close, despite her manoeuvres and attempts to get him to look her in the eye.

His eyes began to well up and he blamed it on the smoke. Xander removed the cigarette for a moment and rubbed the tears away, yet still managed to keep Cathy mostly out of his field of view.

"I loved Sara," he said finally, barring his lip to keep in from shaking. "Julie was just... more convenient."

"This may shock you Xander, but it is possible to love more than one person at a time," she soothed, finally catching one of his hands between both of hers. She rubbed it with both her thumbs. "Like the way I love you and Mike."

"I didn't love her," he spat as he finally turned to look at her. Anger and pain drenched his voice and his nostrils flared. "I didn't. Maybe I thought I did, but I was wrong. You, I love. Sara. Mandy was lovable. Julie was difficult. She was unattainable. She was something I could chase but never have... basically something to occupy my time that went just a little bit too far. So, in other words... she was convenient."

"Just about anything's more convenient then a dead bitch," Tommy said as he sauntered over.

The three of them turned, their gazes following the looks and stares that the words had left in their wake, until they found the person who'd spoken them.

Everyone was silent for a moment. It seemed like even the deep fryers in the back had been hushed by the words, too shocked to form a coherent sentence. When it came time for someone to finally break the silence, it was Mike that found the words first.

"What did you just say?"

Tommy smirked as he leaned back on his chair and popped two chocolate chunks into his mouth. His voice was soothing yet venomous, like a combination of charmer and snake. "Well, Michael, I overheard Alexander and Catherine talking about the former's recent romantic woes, terrible bit of luck that it was. I distinctly heard Xander state repeatedly that Julie was more convenient. That lends to the thought that, to be more convenient, she had to be more convenient than someone else. Since the only other candidate is Sara... that makes a lot of sense. I mean, Julie puts up less fight getting her into bed then a dead girl, after all."

Again there was a silence. He had somehow managed to make his original statement even ghastlier.

Xander took a step forward. His smoke dropped from his lips and landed against his shoe, sending little sparks in all directions before it rolled away. His eyes were transfixed and wide. Another step forward, less slow and mechanical this time, brought a great scowl to his eyes. By the third step, he was almost flying through the air at Tommy. Cathy held him back, though she wasn't trying too hard.

"I am going to kill you," he said under his breath, pulling just slightly on Cathy's grip.

"Why not?" Tommy shrugged merrily as he popped more sweets into his mouth, chewing on them even as he spoke and making great smacking noises with every syllable. "Maybe me and Sara could do the undead bedroom squiggly. Then I'll have been in *both* of your girls."

Cathy let go of her grip on Xander.

He took a moment to register his freedom from her grasp, and only half of one afterward to act upon it. He lunged from where he stood, his feet barely touching the ground as he crossed the twenty feet of dead air between he and Tommy in a heartbeat. He grabbed the mocker by the scruff of his shirt and pinned him against the wall, wrinkling and tearing the posters that adorned it.

"I will rip you in two," he said, so low it was barely audible, using every ounce of restraint he had in him not to completely let loose.

"Why? I'm only telling you the truth," Tommy grinned. He wiped some saliva from his chin and then patted it onto Xander's cheek. "Why do you think she wanted to talk with me at the hospital? She wanted to thank me for putting it to her so good. She even slipped me a twenty for it."

Nobody else in the room moved as Tommy watched Xander's face be at war with itself, looking like every emotion he was feeling was fighting for dominance. And while everyone else in the room could know what Xander must have been going through right now, nobody else could *understand*.

Nobody else was the Black Womb.

Xander felt pain pulse from the tip of each of the fingers in his left hand, the one that held Tommy to the wall. The one that was irritatingly close to the foolhardy youth's neck. It was pain that could have easily been ceased, simply by giving in to the urge that had been building for years now. The urge to end Tommy Irons.

The urge to pop his claws.

Four-inch retractable claws positioned at the end of each finger, each one made of the same dense bone that was inside his lean, muscular body. His lanky form and loose clothing hid a being of formidable physique, capable of world-class athleticism. Blood filled his mouth as a second row of teeth emerged behind his normal ones: this set razor-sharp and able to regenerate. Shark's teeth. His eyes, although they appeared normal, saw more than anyone else in the room. They saw through shadows and the tricks of light. His hearing was strong enough to perceive Tommy's heartbeats, and to know how calm and relaxed the arrogant prick was about this entire situation. Most phenomenal though was the organ which lay deep within his right side. It had the ability to act as any other organ and heal Xander's body past the point of what was previously thought possible. It could even cover his body in a thick, black liquid armor, transforming him into the thing that stalked the nights and punished evil men.

As Tommy squirmed in his hands, the thought of transforming right then and there and gutting him like a fish became almost too appealing to pass up.

Tommy smiled, waiting to see what Xander would do.

Xander drew back, then felt a firm hand on his shoulder. He turned slightly, just enough to see Mike standing behind him, a somber look on his face. Xander panned around the room a little, seeing Joan, Cathy, and a few other Factory patrons watching and waiting on the outcome.

"Come on, Xander," Mike said, squeezing a little. "Tommy's a jerk. I'd like to hand his face to him, too. But he's not worth this."

Cathy tensed.

Mike kept his hand on Xander, and after a moment Xander began to feel the full weight of it. It felt heavy. "He's not that bad."

Xander sighed, turning back to Tommy, who was still smirking wickedly.

"Yes he is," Xander said after a moment, raising Tommy about two inches higher, much to everyone's surprise -- especially Tommy's.

"Am I the only person who still sees it?" he asked rhetorically. "It's like everyone got used to having him around or something. 'Hah Ha, Tommy did this.' 'Oh my gawd, I can't believe Tommy said that,' and everyone thinks it's all in fun. Fun?" he sighed, almost laughing. "Well, what everyone seems to forget is that this guy is going to grow up and become a *man*. A man that grew up getting away with what all of you let him get away with. Grow up actually being encouraged by most to act this way. And he's going to be one of those truly awful human beings that will do something to one of *your* children and then you'll all get on the evening news like ignorant idiots and say 'Oh, he was always such a nice boy. We exchanged cards every Christmas. I never saw this coming.'"

Xander relaxed his grip on Tommy, who was no longer smiling, and slowly lowered him to the ground. "Well, when it happens, don't forget to mention the guy that warned you of it years before, and you were all too stupid to listen."

Tommy twisted away from Xander's grasp, then chuckled a little as he fixed his collar. He feigned a smile, then walked back to his table, grabbed up another chocolate chunk and put it in his mouth as Xander pulled out another smoke and lit it.

"You're right," he mumbled under his breath as he chewed. "I'm not a nice guy. And it's about time I reminded everyone of that. Especially you, Xander."

Xander snorted. He turned and nodded to Mike as the both of them walked back toward their table, where both Joan and Cathy stood waiting and looking panicked. Xander slumped into a chair, hunching his shoulders as a bittered look came over him.

Mike regarded his sulking friend and shook his head in dismay. "Was all that really necessary?" he asked in a hushed voice as they joined the girls.

Xander avoided his friend's gaze, keeping his eyes locked in his peripheral vision. From the corner of his eye, he saw Julie leaning against the bar, frowning at him. He turned to see her completely, only to realize that there nobody was there.

Cathy's hand went immediately to Mike's, squeezing it softly.

Joan sighed, all but collapsing into her chair as tears formed in her eyes, only to be wiped away by her sleeve as soon as they came. "It's for reasons just like this..." she half-whispered to herself, drawing the attention of everyone else in the room.

Xander turned to face her now, ignoring whatever it was he thought he saw.

Cathy put a hand on Joan's shoulder, which she immediately shoved aside.

"...this town isn't like it used to be. I just can't anymore," she sobbed. "I didn't want to do this with all of you here, but we're going to be closing. For good."

The entire room was silent now, all eyes on her. Except for Tommy. He was still chawing on his wad of chocolate.

"I'll give it a month, just for you kids... but after that, I'm done. The Factory is done."

There was a stillness in the room. An unexplainable quality as each person looked to the next for clues on how to feel, but nobody really knew. This building, under one name or another, had been a part of their lives since before they could remember. It had been a part of their parents' lives. Many of their parents had actually met and had their first dates in this building. Now, for the first time in generations, it wasn't going to be here.

Cathy again put her hand on Joan's shoulder, and this time it was not rebuked, but welcomed.

Amid the mute motionlessness, one man stirred.

Tommy Irons got up from his table, his horrible grin having been wiped from his face, and fixed the collar on his jacket. He walked to the exit, turned to see if anyone was following him, and scoffed when nobody did. He slammed the door behind him, shaking the entire building.

CHAPTER TWO
ARE

Deep in the dark he swallowed hard, tasting blood from his lower lip. He had spent the last two hours rending it to shreds with his own teeth. The metallic taste filled his mouth and he grinned in grim satisfaction, revealing teeth and gums lined with red.

Drawing back his head, he snorted then spat out a large wad of blood and saliva onto his fingers. Laughing, he brought them toward the concrete wall he sat against and made a line straight down, then a semi-circle on the top on the right side with another, smaller line coming off from that. It was the letter R.

He giggled gleefully to himself, spitting more blood onto his hand.

CHAPTER THREE
DEFINITIONS

"Amalgam."

Xander looked up from the file folder that he cradled in his arms and shot a glance at Mike (who had spoken the word), before turning back and continuing to read.

There was a long silence between the two in the dead of the room, Mike's nose buried deep in a folder all his own, one a kind of tanned green color.

Finally, Xander slapped his folder shut and sighed. "Okay, I'll bite," he said, laying his reading assignment aside. "What is it?"

Mike looked up from the file, as if just now realizing that Xander was there. "Amalgam," he said again, leaning in so that Xander could see his records as well. "He uses that word over and over again. In like, every sentence O'Toole describes you with it."

Xander glanced at his own folder, which they had stolen last week from their deceased Guidance Counselor's office after realizing that he had been involved in a plot against Xander and his friends. "He does it in mine, too. What's your point?"

"What does it mean?"

"Amalgam. Distorted. To distort. To merge. Basically a half-image of what was before. It was also a DC / Marvel crossover in the 1990's before Joe Quesada came in and decided that crossovers were lame, in which Marvel and DC heroes merged to form new heroes, which were amalgams of the originals. Most notable are Dark Claw, made by combining Wolverine and Batman, and Spider-Boy, created from Spider-Man and Superboy. As another fun fact, it is a romance term coming from an ancient Greek word that translates to 'emollient.' This matches its term in chemistry where it is a softening agent, usually with Mercury... Perhaps only with Mercury."

"I knew what the word meant. I meant why does he keep using it. It's like he's obsessive compulsive about it or something."

"I think you're reading a little too much into this. Is it possible he just misplaced his thesaurus? Besides, it's a pretty accurate description of my ties to the Black Womb."

Mike let that bounce around in his head for a moment, frowning. "I guess. It just seems like he was trying to tell us something."

Xander picked up his file again, flipping through it. "Mike, the man hypnotized us -- gawd, I feel stupid saying that -- then tried to mind-fuck us all over the course of several months. Me and Mandy most of all. According to what we've found here, he also performed experiments on us at some point, trying to make sure that I actually was the Womb. He also sicked Genblade, the Tees, Zakron, and Circe on us, and was probably a party to more than that before we even showed up on the scene. We also don't have any clue what *future* plans he might have had in store for us that might be waiting just around the corner. That's why we've got to figure out these files, find out exactly what Circe knows about all of us, and see if we can figure out when and where they'll strike at us next."

"You don't think there's even a slight chance that we beat them and now they'll leave us alone?" Mike chuckled.

Xander shot him a look.

"Right, sorry. I forgot I was living in an episode of Passions there for a second."

Outside his window, Xander thought he saw something move between his house and the Johnson's, but he paid little to no attention to it.

Her eyes stared forward at her husband, without feeling or emotion. This wasn't the first time. Neither of them moved and neither of them spoke: they simply lay there and looked at one another in a still silence.

Blood dried all around them and the foul stench of death rose up in heated wafts, coating the curtains and the walls; it was the kind of stink that future tenants would complain about for years to come. Their eyes were shrouded and cloudy, their lips cold and dry.

If Jaylen had been alive, this might have reminded her of the first few moments after their first time making love. She had been more than a little drunk. He'd tell her years later that he had dropped some ecstacy earlier that night while he was out with his friends. The two had been dating for several weeks, after meeting at one of her college orientations. He'd already graduated, but stayed around campus, still clinging to the last strings of his old life. He'd come over that night just to talk, a fact they both maintained over the years that followed. He had lived all the way across town, and it was late, so they both decided that he would stay the night.

When it was over, they had just looked at one another, their eyes dead and cold, not knowing what to feel or say. They hadn't spoken or moved, or even made the effort to take him out... they had just lain there, staring at one another.

If Lee had been alive, he would have been looking at her breasts. He had always loved her breasts, but now they seemed somehow different. It was one of those subtle ways that dead bodies looked so different from ones that are alive. Her breasts no longer moved and bounced when she breathed the way they would if her lungs were still drawing air. The color had already gone out of them, too. She looked more and more like an extremely well-articulated mannequin, positioned in the worst possible way.

The front door creaked open, and there was the sound of heavy footsteps on the floor, scuffing against the mat as they came in.

"Oh my gawd."

In his room, still surrounded by ripped shards of the pictures he had taken over the past few years, Tommy sobbed relentlessly, his entire body shaking. He scooped up the pictures and was tossing them into a burnt up coffee tin, stuffing as many of them down inside at a time as he could. Images of his family and his friends, of lovers and hopefuls, of enemies and idiots, all crammed together in the small pot until there was nothing left but a bare, lifeless room.

Fumbling in his pockets he found a pack of matches, and struck one dramatically. It illuminated his face in the dark room, casting eerie shadows over his features and the walls. After gazing into the flame for a moment, he dropped the match into the tin before it could burn his fingers, and watched as the images began to melt and contort as the fire found each one.

He watched as the fire found an image of Randy and his father, smouldering its way up their bodies until only their heads were left. Eventually those were burned and distorted too.

He wiped the last of his tears away, smiling wickedly.

The Factory was empty now, nothing but cobwebs and dust to keep Joan company as the radio blared some junk in the background that she thought was by Billy Talent, so she tried her very best to ignore it, using it only to drown out the sound of the silence.

She swept her broom against the tiled floors, wondering with each stroke why she was even bothering. It was over. She stared around the room at the posters and memorabilia she'd put up over the years. Pictures of her and Roxanne back when they'd bought the place together, both smiling wide, sitting in one of the corner booths, holding up their glasses of champagne to the camera. For the life of her, she could not remember exactly who had taken that picture, but it was right on the tip of her tongue.

Forcing herself to turn away, she continued to sweep the dirt from her patrons' shoes into a large pile in the center of the room, letting out a heaving sigh that shook her entire body.

It wasn't supposed to be like this. She wasn't sure how or why anymore, but she knew that it was supposed to be different, somehow. The world used to be something brighter, sunnier, and now it was just a dank room filled with dirt and musk.

As she walked by a table she picked up a bottle of cola and tossed it toward a garbage can about ten feet away. It made the odd sound of hollow plastic as it ricocheted off the rim of the can, bouncing to the floor before rolling under a nearby table.

She cursed to herself, then rested her broom up against a chair and walked over to the table.

There was a sound behind her and she turned quickly, expecting to see some teen settling into one of the video game machines that adorned the walls.

There was nothing but the stereo, still blaring out mindless drivel, finally getting toward the end of that insipid song. Scanning the room just once, paying close attention to the shadows and the crevices, she turned back toward the table.

Her bones ached in objection as she bent down on her hands and knees to collect the wayward bottle. As it lingered just out of her reach, she briefly considered adding a recycling bin to the Factory, before reality closed in, squeezing ever tighter on her psyche.

The song finally ended, and she closed her eyes in thanks, wondering why she never listened to anything but this station. After a brief moment with a stuttering DJ who tripped over nearly every word, a new song came on. Its jazzy beginning immediately identified it as Livin' La Vida Loca. She suddenly found herself wishing for Billy Talent again.

"She's into superstition, black cats and voodoo dolls. I've got a premonition, that girl's gonna make me fall..."

She heard that sound again behind her, but couldn't quite put her finger on it. There was also a damp, musty odor in the air that would have driven her into obsessive-compulsive cleaning on any night but tonight. She turned away from the bottle again in an attempt to identify the sound.

A sharp pain erupted in the back of her neck, followed by a warm trickling sensation around it on both sides, down around to her chest. The smell became as overwhelming as the heat of her attacker's breath. She turned as she fell back to the floor, staring wide-eyed as she struggled for breath that would not come, the air lost in the obvious hole in her neck.

In that instant before death, as her murderer's hands wrapped around her shirt and pulled her close, she remembered exactly who had taken the picture...

CHAPTER FOUR
BETWEEN

Xander stared at his hands as he sat between Mike and Cathy against Julie's old locker. He was trying to command the Black Womb, to force its vaunted stealth and bodily control and bend it to his own will, but was failing miserably. It seemed to matter how hard he tried, he could not stop his hands from shaking.

"How did it happen?" Cathy asked finally, her own hands buried in her armpits to try and stop them from being so cold, as she rocked back and forth ever so slightly.

There was an almost tactile silence between Mike and Xander then, as each urged the other to speak first. In times like these, they'd discovered that the wrong words could be the death of you.

"We're not sure," Xander said finally, letting his head fall back against the locker, followed by a reverberating echo from within it. "All we know is that she was killed. That it was... savage... even by the standards we've set over the past few months. That the first blow killed her, and that whoever did it just kept hitting her long after she'd died."

"This wasn't just a murder," Mike nodded, staring at the opposite wall. "This was somebody's idea of a party."

"Maybe," Xander added quickly, raising a finger. "We're not sure of anything yet. From what I've been hearing around town, Joan wasn't the first, which probably means she won't be the last. They haven't released the name of the first victim yet, but they have given Joan's. There has to be a reason for that. We find that reason, and we'll find out why Joan was killed. And by who."

There was a pause as Cathy absorbed all of the information. She opened her mouth as if to speak, stopped, then leaned forward and looked at the both of them. "And what good will that do?"

"What?" Mike whispered, squinting at her.

"What good will come of that?" she reiterated, her eyes a mix of pain and fear. "Are we stopping what's happening? Are we making people die less? Every time we do this, someone else decides that they want to be a serial killer. Julie left because she didn't want a part in this life anymore... maybe we should start thinking of doing the same thing. Just getting out of the way and trying not to get killed."

"Cat..." Mike soothed, placing a hand on her elbow.

"No," Xander interrupted, shaking his head at his friend. "No, she's not wrong. You guys should steer clear of this one. Of every one. I've been saying that since the first time we went out. This is my fight. My vow. You two should never have been --"

"You, too," Cathy stated bluntly, grabbing his chin

and turning him toward her. "This isn't where you should be either. We've got to stop this. We can't just keep leaping into harm's way like this."

"We have to protect --" Mike interjected, only to be again cut off.

"*I* have to protect these people," Xander said, stopping him. "I started this... horror, and I have to be the one to finish it. Otherwise everyone'll end up dead like Julie!"

The three of them fell silent again. Mike and Cathy stared at Xander as his chest heaved up and down furiously.

"Mandy," he corrected, his voice softer now. "You'll end up like poor Mandy."

All three looked down at the floor in front of them, letting out a sigh in near unison.

As people continued to walk past the trio, ignoring them, the friends sat and considered what had just been said.

"Hello, my son," came a calm, gentle voice from somewhere in from of them.

They looked up to see Reverend Robert Gallagher smiling down at them, regarding them with a curt but kind nod, his hands clasped in front of him.

"Father?" Xander said, speaking first, scrambling to his feet.

"Hello, Mr. Drew," said the man as he extended his hand, which Xander accepted. The younger man's skin grew goose-bumps at the older's soft touch, and he thought he felt the Womb deep inside of him twitch, just once, ever so slightly. "It's been a long time since I've seen you in my confessional."

Mike regarded Xander with a quizzical glance as both he and Cathy rose to their feet as well, smiling politely at the Reverend.

"Yes..." Xander agreed, finding himself feeling more than a little sheepish. "I am sorry. I always mean to, but can very rarely find the time."

"I still see you up in the graveyard every couple of days. It would do you well to come in some time and talk. And just so you know... we are still open on Sundays."

Xander almost laughed at that, then turned his head toward his friends. "This is Mike Harris and Cathy Kennessy," he said quickly, realizing that he had failed to introduce them.

"A pleasure," Mike said under his breath, shaking his hand just as Xander had.

"The same," Gallagher smiled, then turned to Cathy. "And you I know. I was there at your confirmation... if I do recall."

Cathy almost blushed, then leaned in to give the man a quick hug. "What brings you here?" she asked once they'd parted.

"Actually..." he smiled, although his gaze shifted from them for the first time since the beginning of the conversation.

"You did," came a decidedly less comforting, whiny voice from down the hall. Principal Shnieder walked toward them in his typical marching stance, the lights gleaming off his nearly bald scalp.

Mike raised an eyebrow. "How's that now?"

Shnieder smiled wide, also shaking the Reverend's hand. "Thank you for coming," he said, before turning back to the students. "All of you, actually. He's come by to lend this school a hand in her time of need, and we all thank him very much for it."

The three of them exchanged the same look, then turned back again.

"How's that?" Mike repeated, making it clear that Shnieder had in no way answered the question.

"I'm going to be the new Guidance Counselor," Gallagher smiled, again clasping his hands before him.

Xander's nostrils flared at the thought of it, his eyes darting toward Mike, who he could tell had the exact same feeling. "Well," he said, plastering on a fake smile. "That's just super."

CHAPTER FIVE
AWOL

"Stab wound number three, victim one," he sighed, leaning in close, bending and twisting the overhanging light to get a better look at the wound in question. Lance Berkshire used tweezers to scrape congealed blood into a clear plastic bag and sealed it tight.

He had been a forensic pathologist at Coral Beach Precinct Morgue for almost ten years, and in the last three months, the sheer number of dead bodies he had seen easily tripled. Behind him, his associate Harry Ford performed a similar action on one of the wounds sustained to victim number two: a middle-aged male named Lee Piercey. The victims had been husband and wife.

"What have you got?" Harry asked as he went over the body systematically with a large magnifying glass, using the system that had taken him years to hone and perfect. "Anything probative?"

Lance squinted. "This wound... all of them, they're... very odd."

Harry looked up. With the number of cuts and stabs

the pair suffered; he was surprised to hear Lance say that anything was odd. "What's so weird about them?"

"Well..." he sighed again, placing a hand against her cold body to help him get a closer look, "Most wounds move in some kind of order, depending on the direction of the blade and the position of the killer: right to left, and more importantly, deep to shallow. The depth of the slice isn't consistent."

"And hers is?" Harry asked, removing something from Lee's body, putting it into another plastic bag, then labeling it carefully with a felt tipped marker.

"No. Far from it, actually," he almost laughed and then stopped himself self-consciously. "It starts shallow, then goes deeper... then becomes shallow again. Like a letter V. If I didn't know better, I'd say it was a straight stab, but it doesn't match any of the other weapon marks we've seen on either victim."

"You saying there was another weapon, used for just one blow... or maybe she was forced against something in the house, a corner or something? Gimmie a hand, will you?"

"No, I don't think," Lance said, getting up and moving over to Lee's side with Harry. "I think the killer made it that way purposely, like he was playing... you know? There's no bruising around the wound and it's pale, it was post-mortem... I really think the killer was just playing doctor."

"Creepy," Harry agreed, putting two hands under Lee. Lance did the same. "Three!" Harry said at once. They'd done this so many times no explanation or further count was needed. They rolled Lee over onto his back to continue their autopsy. The back was caked in blood and bile, shaped into the pattern of the floor due to the amount of time he had spent on it.

Lance's eyes went wide, and Harry stepped back a pace as they both saw it, clear as day, imprinted on Lee's upper right shoulder.

"I think I know why they haven't released the names of these two yet," Harry said.

Tattooed on Lee's shoulder was a bright red letter T.

"They don't want to alarm the family."

ᚲᚷ

"Omega," Cathy said simply, taking the buckle out of her hair as she did and placing it on Xander's night table. Her hair immediately fell in front of her eyes, as it always did when not restrained, and she quickly brushed it back behind her ear with one smooth motion of her fingertips.

The radio played 'Have a Nice Day' by Bon Jovi just low enough so that they could hear it, keeping the awkward silences to a minimum.

Xander looked up from his file folder, which contained a detailed account of the Anti-Womb and the events surrounding it, and stared at her. She looked so cute, her legs crossed Indian-style, a folder in her lap, looking down at it as she took a bite of her Crunch bar. "You and your bo... somebody's gotta start talking to you about speaking in full sentences."

"No..." Cathy huffed, getting up and moving over next to Xander on the bed. "This is it. He's talking about the Tees and the Omegas... and the Snakes, whatever they are."

"Rival gang here in town. Only a few members. Nothing like the Tees. They pretty much just steal from grocery stores. Bumped into one or two here and there. Nothing to write home about."

"Ah," Cathy nodded, continuing. "Anyway, this is it. This is where he talks about the deal he made with Randy... I think."

"You think?"

"His handwriting's all lopsided here... and every second word is misspelled, misused, or misplaced."

Xander took the file from her for a second, bringing it to he nose and taking in the scent of it. "He was drunk. It stinks of Rye and Coke. And a little Vodka."

"Ugh," Cathy grimaced, taking the folder back. "Anyone ever tell you that that enhanced senses junk can be majorly creepy sometimes?"

Xander turned toward her, inhaling deeply, his nostrils flaring. He calmly turned back to his own file. "Mike got to third base with you last night on the couch in his basement. There was a scented candle. Vanilla."

Cathy's mouth dropped, and she slapped him once. "Isn't it some kind of super-hero rule that you can't use your powers like that?"

"You don't need super-human senses to see somebody's tongue hanging out, or them wearing the same clothes they did the night before," he mumbled calmly.

Cathy grinned. "Any*way*."

"Yes. Something about the Tees?"

She nodded, fixing her hair again, then went back to the file. "It talks a lot about how he approached them; how he told Randy about you."

"Just Randy, right?"

"Uh-huh. Part of the deal. It doesn't say why."

"Doesn't need to. He's a scientist. Needed controlled variables. Too many people knowing messes up all his equations, and then the experiment doesn't work out the way he thought."

"Which it didn't anyway."

"He didn't count on Genblade waking up. None of us did."

"Mmm," she hummed in agreement. "Then it gives us..." she stopped, eyes growing wide.

"What?" Xander said, almost not paying attention, looking over notes on the Anti-Womb by one of its original creators. "What does it say?"

Cathy sat up straight in the bed, her eyes dancing over the page wildly, trying to take in all of the information on it at once. "It's a list of all of the Tees and Omegas."

Xander sat up so quickly that if she'd been looking at him, she still would not have seen him. He looked over her shoulder at the list, which stretched onto the next page.

"How can there be so many?" she said, more to herself than to him.

"You'd be surprised what people are capable of," he growled. "Especially when there are enough others doing the exact same thing. Mob mentality and all that. If you're part of a group, you're not the one doing the damage -- It's the group. No blame, no guilt."

"Justin Langley, Sven Douglas, Ian Char, Duncan Coombs, Quintin Travers, Randy Owchar, Terrance Owchar, Elliot Piercy, Steve Matthews, Dwayne Piercey, Ryan Matthews, George Walker, Jason Moony, Danny

Quire, Nicolas Sharp..."

"Wait," Xander stopped, pointing at the last few she read. "I don't recognize those last ones."

"There's a red mark on them... it's on George Walker, too. Kerri's dad. Maybe that's a mark for Tees that are no longer active members, one's that quit?"

"You don't quit the Tees," Xander mumbled, taking the folder away slowly. "They quit you. They tell you when you've had enough." He looked long and hard at the symbol marking each of them. It was a circle with twisted lines coming out of the bottom of it, and looked almost like a squat up stick man. "And I've seen this before somewhere... in the files." He turned the page and saw a list of at least forty more Tees, all with the same red symbol next to them. He scanned down the list quickly, eyes fluttering. "I know a lot of these people... my Mom plays bridge with some of them."

Cathy stopped at one name, pointing to it. "Lee Piercey. Why does that one sound so familiar?"

"Dwayne's cousin," Xander responded. "Family ties, which isn't surprising. It can't have just been Randy that was a legacy. This type of bigotry is passed down through generations. I always thought that might be the case, but there was never enough for me to act." He clenched his lower lip.

The radio stopped on some mid-90's Bryan Adams song mid-beat, interrupting with the familiar chime that preceded all that station's news broadcasts.

"Following another possibly-related death in the town of Coral Beach, police have released the names of two victims from last night's murders. Jaylen and Lee Piercey were found dead in their own home…"

Xander and Cathy shot looks at one another, staring at Lee's name on the list. "My god…" Xander sighed. "It's starting again, isn't it?"

"I don't know," Cathy frowned. "But somebody sure seems like they want it to."

∧⟨〉∧

The sun was almost down when Mike opened the back door to The Factory. He did it in the same careful way he'd watched Agent Tim White do it, so as to not arouse police suspicions. Very slowly and calmly, he shut the door behind him to avoid the click of the old lock.

It did anyway.

The sound reverberated off of the walls back and forth until it seemed to be coming at Mike from all directions.

He turned around slowly, looking at the place where he'd spent so many nights, just hanging out or playing pool or hitting on girls. It all looked the same: the posters, the games, the tables… everything. That surprised him more than anything had in a long while. He had expected it to be different, to be tainted or stained with the act that had occurred here, but it wasn't. Each one of the games still hummed away, playing their sound clips and voice-overs, inviting people to come and play them.

He sighed and adjusted his jacket, which had been bunching in the back the whole way over, then walked toward the bar. As he got closer, he could see the outline of white tape that the police had left to mark where Joan's body had been, not that it was needed. The large, human shaped void in the pool of blood was a sufficient reference

Gang War

point.

Careful not to step in anything, he knelt down next the where she must have lain for her last few moments, looking at the redness that surrounded it. He followed one trail that went up and to the right, noting where it splashed on the stools, then onto the bar itself, the Beatles poster on the wall, and finally created a splash or two on the ceiling. He followed the trail back down, his eyes scanning every last droplet.

His brow scrunching as he began picturing the murder, Mike leaned over the body the way the killer must have. He cupped an imaginary knife and began slashing at the air just above the chalk line. Craning his neck, he watched the direction his arm went in after every slice, trying to calculate where castoff from the weapon would go. It completely bypassed the bar, and would have ended up across Van Morrison's face.

Adjusting the angle at which he struck to a backhanded slash, he watched where the blood went now. Across the bar, onto the Beatles poster, and depositing one or two drips on the ceiling. He allowed himself a smile.

Glancing to the left, he saw two more distinct blood trails, and tossed his pretend blade from one hand to the other before repeating the same series of motions. Again it worked, sending the castoff in the exact direction the blood actually went.

He stood again, unclenching his hand in the process, and stepped away to follow the third trail. It didn't go far, and it didn't go up. Instead it stayed on the floor, away from the walls, not like the others, until it reached the corner. Then, it turned. There was a single drip on the other side of the corner. Turning to look at where he'd walked from, Mike imagined himself walking again, holding the knife... blood dripping from it onto the floor, shaking the last bit off as he turned the corner. He looked up the wall, seeing the tiniest smear on the ledge of a still open window.

Again, he smiled a little. Just a little.

"Oh man! You did great!" came a whiny voice from behind him, and he turned quickly, fists clenched and ready.

He was standing face to face with a Marvel vs. Capcom arcade game, which was displaying a list of top scores, scrolling across the screen in blue flashing letters. He walked over to it slowly, the light from the screen bathing his face in blues and reds. The violence on the screen reflected in his eyes and took him back to a time not so long ago, when he wouldn't have had to do things like this.

ᚷ

-clack, crack!-

He pressed the pinky of his right hand against the palm of his left, cracking the bone and feeling the slight rush as pressure released from the joints. He grinned slightly as he sat on the edge of his bunk, moving from one finger to the next, cracking his knuckles, and looking forward at the bars of his cell.

The cell bar's shadows made lines across his tanned, cracked face as he glared silently into the hallway outside. The smooth, clean walls taunted him, as he yearned to simply open the door and step out into freedom.

A stiff breeze came through, bringing with it the familiar stench of urine that one never got entirely accustomed to, making all the hairs on both his massive arms stand on end. He sniffed back a glob of mucus, spitting it as far into the hall as he could, then wiped his mouth with the sleeve of his orange jumpsuit. It was ripped and torn in places from too many fights in the prison yard, so many that they now only allowed him access to it at certain times when there weren't as many inmates. When it was just him and the crazies -- the ones they didn't mind seeing ripped limb from limb. Hell, the guards set up an online shop where they sold security footage.

One such tear was right over his heart. Some punk kid from the next cell over had given it to him with a homemade shiv fashioned from an old toothbrush. From the smell of the little bastard, it had been all he'd ever used the toothbrush for. Though the fabric was ripped, one could still see most of the letters of his name, but not all: Char.

Terrence Owchar.

But that wasn't what they called him, and it wasn't what that kid had yelled right before he lunged at him.

He had called him Roulette.

Xander poured steaming hot water onto some oats, brown sugar, and apple slices, watching as the steam rose up from the concoction slowly, turning it into mush. He flared his nostrils and breathed deep, taking in as much of the aroma as he could.

"That smells so good," Cathy said from her spot against the window at the kitchen table, practically salivating as she spoke.

"Your favorite," he smirked, adding a little canned milk, followed by the slightest squirt from a re-sealable bag of sweetened condensed milk that his mom didn't think he knew about. Taking a spoon out of a nearby cupboard, he stirred it quickly, until most of it looked the same; its various ingredients spaced evenly throughout the blue bowl that had long ago been deemed Cathy's bowl when at this house. He placed it down in front of her, and she quickly ran her fingers through her matted black hair, forcing it behind her shoulders to avoid making a mess while she ate.

"Thanks," she replied honestly, as she picked up the spoon and dug in, trying harder than one would expect for a bonus apple slice. "Been a while since we've done this."

Xander smirked and set down a glass of cold milk on the place-mat as he sat on the chair opposite her. "Too long," he agreed, then raised his glass to her in a pretend 'cheers' before downing its entire contents.

She frowned at him. "That's not all you're having, is it?"

He nodding, laying down the glass. "Don't need to eat, remember? Only reason I'm even having this is my throat feels dry."

She smirked.

"What?"

"Do you realize I slept on top of you last night?" she asked, taking another spoonful of oatmeal, this time getting one of her much-sought apple slices.

"Yeah..." he trailed, blushing a little. "How about we leave that part out when Mike asks where you were last night?"

"Not that, silly. You didn't... you know... go out."

Xander smiled and started watching his fingers dance along the edge of his glass, trying to avoid eye contact with her. "You noticed that too, huh?"

"How long has it been, since the last time you went out at night without trying to?" she asked as she leaned forward excitedly, her hair falling off her shoulders again.

"At least a week and a half, but I think its been more. A lot more. I just only really started noticing enough to pay attention a week and a half ago. I also don't notice it... I dunno, twitching?... for no apparent reason anymore. It's like..."

"Like you're getting control."

Xander smirked, again looking down at the table.

"Why didn't you tell me?"

"Didn't wanna jinx it. Plus, I don't get to see you as much anymore. You've got Mike, and I've been spending a lot more time with..." he trailed off, his voice growing dim as the smile slowly faded from his lips. "You've got Mike, so we haven't been seeing each other as much anymore."

She sighed, reaching out a hand to touch his. "It's her loss, you know. Any girl would be lucky to have you."

He finally met her gaze head on, as her thumb rubbed the tender flesh between his thumb and forefinger, sending shivers up and down his spine.

Inside him, the Womb flinched, making him adjust his position uncomfortably.

"Any girl would," she repeated, bending her head down to reestablish their line of sight.

"Sara used to say that, too," he said glumly. He took a long pause, then got up and brought his glass to the sink to rinse out. "Is it some kind of girl code, or something 'I think you'd make a lot of girls happy, but not me and not anyone I know?'" He sighed.

"That's not it at all," Cathy pleaded as she dug her spoon back into her breakfast.

"Isn't it?" he almost snapped, but stopped himself and pursed his lips. "It seems like everyone wants me to be with someone, that everyone thinks I'd make this amazing boyfriend, but no girl will actually give me the chance to be it. And you know why? Because we both know that I make one crappy fucking boyfriend, Julie."

She looked like she was about to say something, then stopped and tilted her head to one side.

"...Cathy," he amended, leaning against the counter as if it were all that were holding him up. "We both know it."

"Oh, is that so?" she smirked, almost laughing.

"What's so funny? Ha hah, Xander's in pain?"

"No, it's..." she motioned down at her cereal bowl with her spoon. "We're not even together, and look at this. You spent all night snuggled up with me in your arms and never once even tried something that could in any way be considered a move, you get up and make me my favorite breakfast, you talk to me about what's on your mind... Xander, you're right, you wouldn't make a good boyfriend. You'd make an amazing boyfriend. And if you think I wouldn't take full advantage of that if anything happened between me and Mike..." she let that sentence fall off, not needing or wanting to finish it. "It's just that things keep getting in the way. You have to choose not to let them."

Xander nodded, smirking at her. But his eyes looked distant, lost in some horrible thought.

"What is it?"

"Something Julie said. When she left," Xander sighed, rubbing the bridge of his nose. "She said that it wasn't Sara... that it wasn't that I still love her, in ways that I couldn't love Julie. That it was what I really love more than anything. Said that I love death and as long as I do, death will keep following me, wherever I go, and that she couldn't be a part of that anymore."

Cathy let those words hang in the air for a moment, picking her time to speak carefully. The right words said at the wrong time right now could mean the difference between closing up the walls he had around his heart again, something that could take months to undo. "Do you think any part of that's true?"

He looked up at her, and she expected to see tears in his eyes, but there were none. "I think it's all true. I think she's right... and more than that, I think you were right."

She grinned mischievously to herself. "I'm always right," she said coyly. "But, be more specific, which part?"

"Back at the school, before Gallagher interrupted us. I think you were right. After this one... I'm finished. I've got control now. I've avenged Sara's memory a hundred times over... I'm done. This is the end of the Black Womb."

Her eyes went wide, her smile spreading from ear to ear. "Are you serious?"

"More than I ever have been. If I'm going to make it

work with Julie, or the next girl that comes along, I've got to stop seeking death out. If I need to, I'll be able to stop it... but I'm through looking. This is it."

She smiled wider than she'd ever thought possible, then helped herself to another mouthful of oatmeal.

The knob of the front door squeaked, and boots stamped on the mat in the porch.

Cathy threw a look at Xander, who gave the same one back in return. His parents weren't supposed to be back for hours.

Mike walked past the entrance to the kitchen, heading toward the stairs to Xander's room.

"Hey!" Cathy called after him, making him turn and notice the both of them at the table, "What's up?"

"What do you mean, 'what's up?'" he asked, breathless, looking as though he had just run the entire distance from his house to Xander's, which he probably had. "What are you guys doing just sitting here? Don't either of you turn on a tv or radio? Ever?"

Xander's brow furrowed, and he stood just a little straighter, a little taller. Cathy had seen this happen before, a change more dramatic than the one between Xander and the Womb. The walls were back up again, and now it was all business. "What's going on?"

Mike huffed, still trying to catch his breath. "This just became bigger than we thought it would."

CHAPTER SIX
GANG WAR

Xander stood back from the cell, with Mike not far behind him. A few feet further down the narrow corridor police tape sectioned it off from the other cells, wrapped around on of the bars and held in place firmly with sticky tack. He could see it all, but for some reason still felt the need to step closer. With every step he grew more and more repulsed, disgusted... and oddly peaceful. There was a sense of closure in the bleak concrete walls.

Though police procedure was often lax to the point of ridiculousness in Coral Beach, when the tape was up Xander had learned to mind it. He'd never really noticed any fault with the justice system in his corner of Maine before a few months ago. But then, he'd never been exposed to any real issues before then either. He had been blissfully ignorant, it the same fashion that he now described the officers themselves. He'd noticed it first just after the Engen Corporation kidnapped him. While the surviving kidnapper had been (and was still) behind bars, the building itself had never been thoroughly investigated, to the point that several items left behind continued to cause havoc even weeks later. Things had gotten so bad that, after helping out one too many times (catching Darren Phillips, assisting in the search for Kerri Walker, and successfully finding Charles Frank, to name a few) there was now an open door policy between Xander, Mike, and the Coral Beach Police Department. Of all the times he'd felt the urge to comment on the issue, this was not one of them.

Blood ran down the drain in the center of Roulette's cell, making a tiny dripping sound that only Xander could hear. The stench was unimaginably potent, coming at him from all sides. He swallowed back a glob of bile as he nodded curtly to Warden Tim Greyson. He stretched his fingers until they cracked, then took the last step forward until his midsection pushed against the police tape.

The floor of the cell was drenched in blood. Against the bunk on the adjacent wall was a void in the almost-black redness, distorted slightly by the absorbing effect the mattress had. There hadn't been an outline done yet, but the body had been removed.

"Couldn't have happened to someone more deserving," Mike said coldly, stepping in behind Xander, crumpling his nose and bringing a hand to his face briefly. "Lord, how can you stand that smell?"

"Barely notice it," Xander sighed. He reached into his jacket pocket and produced a thinly rolled cigarette, placed it between his lips quietly, lit it, then took a long drag. "I can still smell it on Cathy from the... from a few months ago. It's everywhere for me now."

They both stepped along the edge of the tape, until they could see further into the cell and the bunk came fully into view. In the center on the void where Roulette's body had been there was an oval-shaped yellow mark, mostly faded.

"Guy went and pissed himself," came the Warden's voice as he walked by, glancing in at the two. "Made one hell of a mess in his trousers, too. Just be glad we removed the damn thing. An hour ago, you couldn't step in there without a mask on."

Xander nodded without turning toward the man, then crouched down until he could see under the tape that blocked their path. Mike raised an eyebrow, about to ask him what he was doing, then thought better of it. Instead he examined the blood spatter that ran up the walls from the direction of the body. The droplets were pointed upward, meaning the killer was hunched over Roulette when he'd been slashing away at him. He imagining the blade again, like he'd done back at The Factory. "He did it back-handed again," he mumbled to himself.

"Did what backhanded?" Xander asked, flicking the remains of his cigarette out the cell window.

"The cuts the killer made, they were all backhanded. Like at the Factory."

There was a noise somewhere to the left, and both men froze. After a few seconds of silence, the two resumed. "How do you know what kind of strokes the killer made at the Factory?"

Mike paused a moment, pretending to examine a particularly large blood drop to avoid his friend's gaze. "Police report. I've still got some friends here in the department from when me and White took down Phillips."

There was a noise again, almost like the creek of

springs, and Xander swallowed hard; his mouth went dry for no reason at all. "Ah," he said, pretending he hadn't heard anything. "So, we're pretty sure this was the same guy, right?"

"Mm-hm," Mike hummed, glancing at the grated window to see if there were similar smear marks on it, like when Joan was killed. "I don't know about the police, but there's no doubt in my mind that we're dealing with one guy."

"He didn't move," Xander said finally, standing up.

"What?"

"He didn't get up from his bunk. Guy as big as Roulette, didn't even try to defend himself. Killer had to open the lock, open the door, come across the cell, stab him (repeatedly)... and he didn't move. Didn't even fall or slump over after he was dead. Just stayed there."

"Maybe he didn't think he had something to be afraid of," Mike offered. "Maybe he knew the guy, or it didn't seem threatening. You getting any scents?"

Xander closed his eyes and tilted back his head, breathing in deep through both his nose and his mouth. "Too much blood, can't get anything decent. It's all covered in his scent. There is something though, but I can't put my finger on it...."

"But it's familiar," Mike finished for him, seeing where it was going.

"Very. Whoever it is, I've met him before. I just don't know from where," Xander agreed, twitching his nose to try and get the foul smell out. "Come on, we've learned all we will here."

Mike nodded, turning toward the cell door.

The two of them rounded the corner back out into the halls, then stopped.

The cell next to Roulette's was dark and shadowed. The light that hung from its ceiling had been broken and the barred window covered shut somehow. Both men looked into it. Not a sound came from it, but there was somehow a loudness in the silence. It screamed.

There was a shuffle in the darkness, and something that could almost be called a giggle.

Deep inside of Xander, the true Womb surged violently, so hard that he thought he might throw up or just plain keel over right there on the floor.

"Come on," Mike said, unable to take his eyes away from the cell while they stood next to it. "Cathy's waiting out in the lobby."

〽

"Well, that was useless," Mike grumbled, as the trio walked by the playground on their way back to Xander's house, trying not to look in at the children playing in the snow and slush. "Did you learn anything from the officer out front?"

"No," Cathy drawled, looking a little disappointed in herself. "The security cameras didn't catch anything, but the view of Roulette's cell is distorted in all the tapes anyway. Don't know why they wouldn't have better surveillance over the cell of a gang-lord who just happened to be a rapist and murderer."

"Simple," Xander said harshly, finally speaking up. "So that when somebody finally got up the balls to kill him, they'd have an excuse not to catch the guy."

Cathy looked shocked at the response, then remembered how many policemen had been killed by Tees over
the years, and realized the idea made sense. "So, what
about you guys? Are we any closer to finding out who
this creepola is and getting it over with?"

Xander smirked at her briefly. The use of the word
'creepola' reminded him that not everything in this world
was dark and black.

"We think it's someone we've encountered before,"
Mike piped up, tapping his nose twice and then motioning in Xander's direction.

"And it's becoming pretty clear that they have some
kind of grudge going on against the Tees. So, let's start
there."

"Well, there's the three of us, and Julie," Cathy
frowned, only half meaning the words coming out of her
mouth.

"Tommy's got a pretty big mad-on for all those gang-
types," Mike added, tightening his fists.

"Mm," Xander thought. "There's also the Circe. They
seem like the type who like to tie up loose ends, and they
definitely have the means to pull off something like this,
even if you don't count Zakron into the equation."

Cathy's eye twitched at the mention of Zakron, but
she said nothing on the subject. "Then there's that Sebastian jerk. We never did hear from him again, and we don't
really know what he was all about."

"We've also got a list of former Tees and Omegas about
a mile long back at the house. Any one of them could have
a reason to pull a stunt like this."

Mike frowned, looking thoughtful. "I dunno. I feel

like we're getting further away from it here. Sure, all these people have reasons to go after the Tees... but who would want Joan dead?"

Joan sighed, all but collapsing into her chair as tears formed in her eyes, only to be wiped away by her sleeve as soon as they came. "It's for reasons just like this..." she half-whispered to herself, drawing the attention of everyone else in the room.

Xander turned to face her now, ignoring whatever it was he thought he saw.

Cathy put a hand on Joan's shoulder, which she immediately shoved aside.

"...this town isn't like it used to be. I just can't anymore," she sobbed. "I didn't want to do this with all of you here, but we're going to be closing. For good."

The entire room was silent now, all eyes on her. Except for Tommy. He was still chawing on his wad of chocolate.

"I'll give it a month, just for you kids... but after that, I'm done. The Factory is done."

There was a stillness in the room. An unexplainable quality as each person looked to the next for clues on how to feel, but nobody really knew. This building, under one name or another, had been a part of their lives since before they could remember. It had been a part of their parents' lives. Many of their parents had actually met and had their first dates in this building. Now, for the first time in generations, it wasn't going to be here.

Cathy again put her hand on Joan's shoulder, and this time it was not rebuked, but welcomed.

Amid the mute motionlessness, one man stirred.

Tommy Irons got up from his table, his horrible grin having been wiped from his face, and fixed the collar on his jacket. He walked to the exit, turned to see if anyone was following him, and scoffed when nobody did. He slammed the door behind him, shaking the entire building.

"Tommy," Xander said, growling deep inside his throat. "It was Tommy."

Cathy nodded, shocked at the fact that she wasn't shocked. That it sounded true; sounded right. "Tommy," she said aloud, and it felt correct.

"I dunno," Mike said, stopping in his tracks. "I mean, no doubt the guy has been a jerk lately, but murder? That's a bit of a jump."

Xander met his friend's gaze with something resembling frustration, though much more intense.

"A bit of a jump?" he barked. "It wasn't even four months ago that this guy beat you over the head with a piece of two-by-four to help his friend rape Cathy. That he was chummy with not one but all of the Tees, whether he knew what they were or not, plus his best friend was an Omega. He had that crush on Mandy he couldn't let go of, then the Tees killed her... who else could it be?"

Mike put his hands into the air, relenting. "All I'm saying is that maybe we should wait a little while before going after the fucker with guns blazing. We don't want to make any mistakes here, right?"

Xander squinted. "And while we're waiting, more people are going to end up dead. Maybe you. Maybe Cathy, depending on how pissed off the little dick is at everybody. No..." he trailed off, shooting a glance at Cathy. "...we end this now."

Cathy paused, then nodded in agreement. "Not without me. Not this time."

Xander nodded curtly. "I think it's time we showed

Mr. Irons what a Black Womb is capable of."

Mike huffed. "Fine, I just... there's some stuff I want to check on first, okay? Can this wait until later tonight?"

Xander threw a glance and Cathy, who simply shrugged her shoulders. "We'll go to my place and wait until ten. After that, we're going after him, and we're not stopping until we get the truth out."

Mike nodded, gave Cathy a kiss, then went off the other direction -- toward The Factory.

Warden Greyson peered out between the blinds of his office window, glancing quickly from side to side.

"Any sign, sir?" came the voice of a much younger officer, who still had a bit of an acne problem across the forehead, and tried to hide it unsuccessfully with long bangs.

"No," Greyson replied, turning from the window and letting the plastic snap shut, killing the lone streak of light in the otherwise dark room. "But you never can tell with those kids. That Harris especially. Shows real promise. Hope he decides to join the force some day, if he keeps his nose clean and manages to keep himself alive."

The younger cop -- with a badge that read Lanus-- nodded, looked down and remembered the thick file folder in his hands, then placed it on the Warden's desk.

"Do they know anything?"

Greyson took a long sip of his coffee, soaking his greying moustache as he did so. "Only what they hear on the news, maybe a little more. They have their suspicions, but right or wrong, they don't know the scope of it yet."

Lanus stood quietly for a moment, mumbling a little,

choosing his words carefully. "With all due respect sir, why aren't we telling them everything? The media, I mean?"

Over the brim of the Warden's cup, Lanus saw the older man's eyebrows raise.

"Son," Greyson started, putting his cup down. "A dead gang-lord is bad enough before you take into account that it happened while he was under our protection. *Thirty-eight* missing Tees with enough blood at each scene to tell us they were killed, yet no body in sight? Now that's pushing it. I'm just glad Harris bought my story about moving Owchar's body -- they didn't need to know the killer managed to drag it away without us or the cameras seeing it."

"Sir... what are we dealing with here?"

"It's a gang war, son," Greyson sighed, picking up his coffee again. "'Sit next to the river long enough, and the bodies of your enemies will float by.'"

"What was that, sir?"

"Nothing, son."

Mike opened the front door to The Factory again, not taking the time to look around now. He ignored the blood spatter on the walls and the chalk outline where Joan's body had been, moving instead to the pool table where he and Xander had been playing just the other day. Frowning down at it for a second, he hopped up and sat against the ripped green fabric. Steadying himself, he took a long pan of the room now, making note of every little thing.

What's different? he thought to himself, trying to force

his brain to work. *You were here just the other day, idiot. The killer must have been, too. Now what's different?* His eyes darted all around, trying hard not to let them focus on any one thing in particular, but on the room as a whole. To see it as one large object and then find the flaw in its composition.

The air felt wrong here, just as it had back in Roulette's cell. Something was out of place, something was different.

"You can't do this, bitch!" Tommy Irons screamed as he drew back the dagger and lashed out in a backhanded slice that ripped open her breasts. She fell to the floor in an awful slump, her head smacking off one of the bar stools. Her eyes were wide with terror.

Mike, frowning, turned and looked at the row of posters behind him. It wasn't back there; everything looked fine. No, something in front of him called out, crying to be seen. Begging for it.

"Beg for it," Sebastian sneered coldly, the gem on his forehead sparkling in the low flourescent lighting, his eyes alive with a glee that his face did not portray. He raised up his sword again, twirling it and slicing through her flesh with each spin, sending long, repetitive tendrils of blood all over the walls.

"I don't even know you!" Joan screamed, holding up an arm in a vain attempt at self defense. "I don't know what you're talking about!"

"The stone! The stone is here, it has to be! Just tell me where the stone is and you can live, witch!"

"No..." Mike sighed, standing up and walking slowly toward the wall, as if narrowing in on what was wrong with the room. He knew it was close now, but still couldn't see it, and the closer he got to the far wall, the more wrong it seemed. Not something added, but something missing.

"Zaaa- Kraonnnn!" Zakron bellowed, thrusting his massive head up into the air; spraying blood from his lips in all directions as its black, oozing face contorted with rows of teeth moving about in its mouth as if they had a will all their own.

Joan screamed as the life drained out of her, watching as the puddle of blood next to her head grew larger and larger, trying to look at anything except the dark beast lingering above her, bobbling from side to side like an animal toying with its prey.

"Zak," it grunted, the breath that jutted out from its nostrils visible in the coldness of the bar area. "Ron." It ripped forward with its massive claws, tendrils whipping around to hold her, to stop her from shaking as its massive tongue draped its way all over her body.

Mike was almost nose-to-nose with the wall now, looking around him. There was a long space with nothing but pictures... one was missing. It had been a picture of Roxanne and Joan on the day they had bought the Factory. Right where it had been, there was one tiny blood smear... far away from any of the others.

"You took it, didn't you?" he asked aloud. "You took it when the blood was still wet on your hands. Why did you want this? What could it have meant to you?"

He touched the bare wall briefly, noticing that it was a slightly less faded brown then the rest from being covered by the picture.

The picture.

Officer Lanus walked past Roulette's cell, gazing in again at all of the blood. He felt bile rise up from his gut as he tried to find one square foot that did not have at least some on it, and found that he could not. And from what some of the other beat cops were saying, this hadn't even been the worst. They said that when the killer had hit some guy named Quire's house, they first hadn't thought there was any blood... until they'd realized that the walls were *painted* with it, a smooth coat smeared over the entire interior of the bedroom.

He got wobbly for a second and gripped the iron bars of the cell for support. His stomach did a back-flip, complete with an accompanying -- and very attractive -- plopping sound. He gasped, sighing just a little as he closed his eyes, took a deep breath, and then opened them again.

Setting his jaw and straightening his shirt, he composed himself and turned to the right to continue his run of the grounds.

"Boo."

A large hand jutted out from the adjacent cell, grabbing Lanus by the collar and pulling him against the bars, slamming his jaw against the cold metal. He screamed, even as a second hand jabbed a light bulb into his eye then twisted, sending dark blood rushing down his face and gathering in his open mouth until he thought he was going to choke on it. The hand released the now-shattered glass, wedged in the young officer's face, reached putrid-tasting fingers into his mouth and then pressed his thumb against his Adam's apple, trying to make a fist while clenching the lower half of the man's face.

The attacker yanked forward with one hard tug, pulling the man's head against the bars. There was a sick, wet snap as the two collided, then he pushed back and pulled again. One side of Lanus' jaw shattered.

Trying hard to scream but finding it very difficult, Lanus' good eye searched the darkness of the cell for any trace of his assailant and found nothing. All of a sudden, he heard a groan, followed by a squeak. He was silent, then, gazing into the darkness for any sign of motion.

There was a flash of something that looked like it might be metal. He felt the sting as sweat billowed from his forehead into his open eye socket.

Something came toward him out of the darkness, swinging at him. It crashed into the left side of his head, jarring it and snapping his neck, his entire body going limp, slumping against the cell.

From within the darkness, there was a small chuckle.

The hands reached forward again, this time patting down Lanus's midsection until they found what they were after. They returned from his body with his weapon, a .357 caliber Glock. The hand fell into the darkness again and came back empty, lingering on Lanus for only an instant before returning with his keys.

Carefully, he found the right one and placed it in the lock to his cell. He turned until he heard it snap open, then slid the cell door to one side, stepping out into the light.

Derek Smith inhaled deeply, pushing his long auburn hair back behind his head. The smile on his face undeniable. His beady little eyes were alive with excitement beneath thick, bushy eyebrows. As he turned his muscular body toward the exit, his finger was already putting first pressure on the trigger finger of the gun.

At the end of the hall, another cop darted around the corner responding to the violence on his co-worker. He was followed by two more, all reaching for their holsters and shouting something at Derek that he was just too happy to listen to.

"Look," he smirked, raising his weapon. "More people want to play."

CHAPTER SEVEN
KILLERS

Xander and Cathy sat in his parents' car, parked across the street from the Tommy's house. The radio was playing something by Three Doors Down, but God only knew what: all their songs sounded alike anyway.

"Can't believe they let you take the car," she said, frowning. "Is this like the time in fourth grade, when Mike 'gave' you his heat-seeking Optimus Prime doll, but you really stole it?"

"First of all, it was not a doll, it was an *action figure*, okay?" he started, pointing at her to enunciate the statement. "Secondly... no." He smiled, gripped his hands around the steering wheel. "No, Dad wasn't going to let me. Then I made up a reason and Mom threw me the keys, gave me fifty bucks and shooed me out the door as fast as she could."

Cathy raised an eyebrow. "What did you tell her?"

"That I was taking a girl out. Which wasn't technically a lie, I suppose, but she's been so 'get back on the horse' about the Julie thing that she didn't even want to know the details. As long as it was a female capable of one day giving her a grandchild, she was happy."

Cathy smirked, tilting her head down to avoid him seeing her blush.

"What?" he chuckled, craning his head toward her. "What is it?"

"Nothing..." she responded musically, almost laughing. "It's just... ah... me and you, and kids, in the same sentence. Can you imagine how weird that would be?" She snorted a little, taking a sip of her drink through her straw and looking out the windshield at the street lights up ahead.

He stared at her for a long moment, the glean of the lights stuck in her hair, making it shimmer, her face palely lit. "Yeah."

He gripped the steering wheel, turning his head away to face forward, letting the radio fill the silence between them.

"It's just you and me, and all of the people with nothing to do... nothing to lose and there's you and me, and all of the people and I don't know why, I can't take my eyes off of you..."

He took a deep breath, then looked down at the glowing green lights of the dashboard clock.

"Nine fifty," he stated bluntly. "Mike's got ten minutes to get here and tell us he's got something, or I'm going in there and kicking some serious ass."

Cathy frowned, staring at the clock herself, then letting her eyes dance over the street, wishing for Mike to come running around the corner.

Xander noticed. "Do you not want to be here? I've got time to swing you home."

Cathy shook her head. "I want to be here. If this is your last time out, I want to be here for it. It's just... the idea of it being Tommy. Someone I called my friend, someone we fought beside."

"Seems a little too familiar, huh?"

"Yeah," she heaved glumly. "I just can't wait for this to be over finally. To get back to some kind of a normal life. I miss worrying about, 'Hey, that guy looks cute. If I wasn't with Mike I'd kiss him. Oh, my gawd, how can I think that? What's the harm in one kiss? Nobody has to know.' Instead, it's, 'Hey, that guy's a serial killer. He's trying to kill my best friend. Oh, wait, everyone I know dies or leaves or becomes a serial killer. Oh, wait, my best friend's the serial killer...' Y'know?"

A smile perked over the corner of Xander's lips. "Who did you think was cute?" he asked, as a slow song by the Backstreet Boys started playing.

Cathy blushed a little and turned away.

His hand danced along the edge of her shoulder, subconsciously playing with the strands of hair that dangled there; hairs that always went off in their own direction despite her best intentions to keep it tame, yet always looking so amazing.

She looked back up at him, her eyes shinny and bright, her lips gleaming against the dashboard display.

At once they leaned into one another, neither of them separately starting it, but instead each finishing the other's motion. Their lips met open-mouthed: her lips soft and supple, his moist and intensely strong. She reached up with both her hands, holding each side of his face and pulling him closer, even as his own hands slid up her

arms, reaching her shoulders and gripping them, dancing between them and the nape of her neck and then back
again. He broke off from her lips and kissed her lower
cheek, then down to her neck as she pulled him closer toward her, on top of her.

-Bing!-

They both stopped, frozen by the sound that came
from the radio, as if it had been the timer on their motion. He leaned back a moment, away from her neck, and
looked at her.

*"That was 'Incomplete' by the Backstreet Boys here on
WCBR1. This is Tara Sampson and we've got lots more of today's hits and yesterday's classics here for you tonight, but now,
here's the news at ten..."*

He looked at her, almost laughing. She looked back up
at him, her hand still rested on the back of his head. She
wasn't laughing.

"This probably isn't a constructive course of action,"
he chuckled, moving off of her. He felt her hand tighten,
and stopped.

"Yes it is," she whispered, pulling him back toward
her. Their lips met again as she wrapped one leg around
him, pulling his entire frame into her.

*"Following an incident at the Coral Beach Penitentiary
that resulted in an unconfirmed number of deaths, the murderer
known as Derek Smith is at large. Residents in the greater area
are urged to stay in their homes."*

Xander shot up in his seat, followed by Cathy, the
both of them forgetting everything that had just happened
a moment ago and sat staring at the radio.

"We will bring you more details as the situation develops.

For now..."

Xander stared the radio, paused for only a moment, then turned the key and felt the engine roar to life.

"What are you doing?" Cathy snapped, grabbing him by the arm.

"Bringing you home," he responded dryly, not even bothering to look at her as he turned around to see if it was clear to pull out.

"Yeah, I'll be safe there," she said, rolling her eyes. "I'm sure Derek doesn't remember where I live. Me, the girl that shot him and put him in jail. I bet he can't even remember my name."

"You're abusing sarcasm at this point," he said in an even tone, and without looking at her. "We're getting you home and I'm getting the cops to come over and watch your place. It won't be a hard sell for them. Then I'm going out and I'm finding Derek, and then I'm going to feed him his intestines. And..." he stopped, turning his head to the left and staring at Tommy's front door. "And by that time Tommy could have killed again."

She frowned, nodding at him and running a finger through the hair above his ear.

His face contorted with frustration as a million thoughts bounded through his head, and he looked as though he were about to cry. "I know, baby," she soothed, stroking the side of his face, "Believe me, I know..."

"Genblade or Randy?" he whispered to himself, staring at the odometer.

"What?"

"I've had to face this kind of choice before.

"Womb!" Hale shouted as Genblade drove the blade for-

ward. It sliced clean through him, spewing blood out through the treads of the sword.

Genblade withdrew and let Hale fall to the ground, still alive. Blood was coming out of the gaping hole in the man's chest. It was so dark and bubbled out so furiously that it looked like oil escaping from a sprung vein, soaking through his clothes and into his skin. He was bleeding to death, and quickly.

"Isn't this interesting?" Genblade sneered, watching the life pump out of Hale's veins. He danced around Hale in a small circle, then leaned down to grin right in his face. "After all this time it's you that's going to fall, not me. Not like you always said. And I'm not even going to give you a decent death, you see that? You're going to die bleeding and mewing like a stuck cat and I'm going to watch. It's over now, do you get that? The Circe is done, do you hear me? Are we clear?"

"Crystal."

Genblade turned just in time to see Xander's claws coming toward his face.

They connected, all four of them ripping a different line through Genblade's skin, like tiny ditches dug for blood to flow through.

"Argh!" Genblade screamed, his head flying forward into his palm as his face burned. "Can't I ever be rid of you?"

"When Mandy died, I had a choice. I could have left and been there in time to stop Randy and save Mandy, but I didn't. I chose to stay and fight Genblade. To rip him open and put him in a hospital bed for the rest of his life. But if I'd left... sure, Hale would have died, but that'd be it. Worst case scenario is that Genblade would have come looking for me again afterward and I would have beaten him then. I made the wrong choice and now..."

"Shh," she cooed, bring his head to her shoulder and stroking it softly. "It's okay. It's oookay."

"I can't make this choice. I can't... I can't do this again. I can't feel responsible..."

"Then let me," she said calmly.

His head rose, and he looked at her, forcing back tears. "What?"

"Let me make this one. Let me decide what we should do, and you just listen. Right or wrong, black or white, I'll take the heat if we fuck this one up. You don't feel any guilt about it either way, okay?"

Xander looked thoughtful for a minute, sniffing back tears, then nodded.

She smiled a little. "It's ten-oh-six. We're late for our appointment with Mr. Irons."

He smiled at her, then turned off the car and opened the door.

Mike stared at the televison screen for a long moment, watching the images dance across them. There was no sound on the black-and-white footage, and yet he could hear each shot that Derek took and feel them sink swiftly into his gut. His lower lip trembled, but he stopped it quickly, raising a hand to his mouth and coughing. He was unable to blink or even to move as he watched Derek leave the building, playfully blowing on the tip of the gun he'd stolen, like a cowboy in some 60's spaghetti western, long hair billowing backward as he opened the front door.

"That's enough," he said after a moment, tearing his

eyes away from the screen long enough to look up at Warden Greyson. The footage was now just an empty hallway, with the body of one police officer half hidden from
the corner camera's view.

Greyson nodded solemnly, pressing stop on the DVR
and ejecting the disk, letting it dangle between his fingers
for a second. "Fuck," he said under his breath. "As if this
town didn't have enough to worry about."

Mike didn't answer, still staring at the screen even
though it was now covered in snow.

The Warden sat down, tossing the tape onto his desk
atop a mound of files and folders. "Derek Smith," he
said in a hushed voice. "Of all people, it had to be Derek
Smith."

"Mm."

"I'm sorry we even have to bring you in on this. Known
acquaintances always get the third degree when anything
like this happens. And you and Derek --"

"We have a history," Mike finished for him, still staring at the blank screen. " I know."

"I don't think we have any more questions. Sorry to
bother you."

"I was coming in anyway. Wanted to take a second
look at Owchar's cell. Something just doesn't seem right
about any of this. It's right on the tip of my tongue..."

"Like a goddamn piece of food stuck in your teeth. You
know it's there, and you can pick at it all you want, but
that fucker ain't coming out until he's good and ready."

"Yeah," Mike sighed, still keeping one eye on the
screen as if expecting it to do something else. In his mind,
it was playing his memories of Derek. When they'd played

together as kids, when Mike had taught him how to win at arcade fighters, when the both of them had worked together to stop Dr. Phillips... when he'd held a knife on Cathy and tried to kill her. When he'd stabbed Xander. When he killed a good percentage of the school and almost got away with it.

Greyson stopped talking and just watched Mike as he mulled things over in his head, letting the thoughts bounce around over and over again.

"I'm gonna wanna see his cell," Mike said finally, reaching out and turning off the screen.

"It hasn't been cleared or swept yet..."

"I'm gonna wanna see his cell," Mike repeated in the exact same tone of voice and manner.

Greyson nodded, reaching for the keys that hung at his side and slowly rising to his feet, moving down toward the containment block.

The pair stepped into the cool, white hall, and Mike was convinced he could see his breath rising up from his nose every time he exhaled. The walls were covered in bloodied hand-prints. He recognized them immediately as Derek's. He had the massive palms of a bear, with tiny, thin fingers. Once the two men turned another corner to get to Derek's and Roulette's cells, Mike stopped dead in his tracks. His mouth dropped open as he turned to face it full frontal, putting his hands on his hips.

Written across the wall, about three feet high and stark against the white primer, was a message written in blood. It said: THE REASON.

"You still wanna see the cell?" Greyson asked, raising an eyebrow.

"I think this'll be good," Mike drawled, mentally shooting the cop a look, but unable to tear himself away from the image to actually do it.

"What do you suppose it means? The *reason*? What's the little bastard talking about?"

"Dunno," Mike shrugged, letting all the air out of his lungs. "But you can damn well bet we're going to find out."

CHAPTER EIGHT
THE REASON

Mike burst out of the police station and bolted in the direction of Tommy's house, cutting across the playground. He was running so fast that his feet hurt already; so badly that he thought they might fall off.

-Squeak!- came a noise from his right, and he turned quickly, his fists clenched and ready to strike.

There was nothing there, just a tire swing swaying back and forth in the winter's breeze. He stayed there, watching it for a second. Back and forth, back and forth.

The Reason? he thought, so loudly that it made his head hurt. *What in God's name is...*

Back and forth, back and forth.

"Maybe I'm not being... direct enough for you."

Back and forth, back and forth, like the gears churning in his mind, the piece of food in his teeth shaking loose and slipping down his throat like poison.

Back and forth, back and forth.

Slowly everything fell into place and Mike's eyes went wide. He turned swiftly on his heels, changing direction, then took off down the street.

I just pray I'm not too late.

Tommy sat in his room, surrounded by broken and torn pictures that he'd taken over the years, watching as half-faces stared back up at him. Their eyes still borrowed into him and their smiles still taunted him, no matter how many times he cut them down.

He let out a long breath and closed his eyes, letting his head slump down a little. The blade he held in his hand shone in the low light of his bedroom, and he felt the cool of the metal between his fingertips. The edges were still stained with dried blood, tiny dots of it congealed around the very tip. It made it look more menacing somehow, transforming it from merely an object into a weapon.

His spiked hair was matted and sticking off around the ears from days of leaving the gel in it, sleeping with it in, and letting the rain get at it. His face was tense and serious. The mouth that was typically drawn upwards in a sly, almost devious grin that had earned him a reputation with the females of the school was now hung low, looking to be almost set in stone there.

"Has it got to you yet?" came a voice from the doorway, familiar, and twisted by anger.

Tommy's eyes shot open and grew twice as wide once he turned toward the speaker. Xander, with hatred burning in his eyes, was half hunched over with his fists clenched so tight that his knuckles were turning white. Cathy was behind him, hanging back but looking ready to move forward at a moment's pause.

Tommy did not respond to the question. He just glared, squinting his eyes a little.

Xander stared back, moving his thumb over his forefinger and cracking it.

"What do you want?" Tommy asked finally, turning away from the pair to face the pile of photos again.

Xander almost laughed. "What do you think, you little runt?"

"Xander-- " Cathy started, but was cut off when Xander raised a hand for silence.

"I'm going to rip you limb from limb," he finished, looking around at the walls, so bare now.

Tommy snorted. "You're not John Wayne, Drew," he said coldly, still not turning to face them.

Xander could see the knife now. He could smell the blood on it from the second he'd entered the house two floors down. "Let's step outside," he said simply.

"Xander--" Cathy repeated, more urgently this time, touching his shoulder.

He shrugged her away, and she realized that, just like in the car, she wasn't talking to Xander anymore. He'd transformed again, into the dark person that always brought a taste of fear to her.

"Leave me alone," Tommy said in a flat, low voice, his head hanging down to look at the blade now, again moving it in the light and watching its glean.

Xander pushed off his heels, moving forward in one fluid motion, like water flowing through the air. Before either party could blink, he had grabbed Tommy by the back of the shoulders and spun him around, slamming him into the wall and pinning him there.

"I will *not* leave you to kill anymore!" he bellowed, gritting his teeth, the Womb rose a little from the outburst but he choked it back, wanting more than anything to do this himself.

"Xander!" Cathy yelled, grabbing his shoulder and digging her nails in, pulling her friend's one arm off of Tommy.

Xander turned to Cathy and snapped, "What?" His face, reddened with anger and hatred, burned even when he looked at her.

She said nothing, just looked past him at Tommy.

A quizzical look came over Xander's face and some (but not all) of the wrath drained out of it. He squinted at her a moment, looking for an answer, then turned back around to see that Tommy was crying.

His eyes were swollen and puffy and his cheeks were wet with hot tears that showed no sign of stopping any time soon. Xander raised an eyebrow, then let his hand slip and fall away from Tommy, who now sobbed uncontrollably. His whole body was shaking and his hands were over his face in a desperate attempt to try and hide it from the world...

... that's when Xander noticed the scars and scabs that lined his wrists and lower arms.

He stepped back from the sobbing youth, backing up a pace or two until he stood on par with Cathy, the both of them looking at Tommy in shock.

"Go ahead..." Tommy sobbed, his whole body shaking. "Just do it. I'm sick of this. Sick. They all die or leave or hurt... now you are too, I can't... I'm so sorry. I'm sorry about the things I said, I just..." he was overcome by sobs then, burying his head into drawn up knees, holding himself in the fetal position.

"You didn't kill Owchar..." Xander whispered, more to himself than to Tommy.

Tommy looked up, his whole face soaked now. "He's dead?" he said quietly, his eyes darting around in their sockets, confused.

"You didn't hear?" Cathy said in a soothing voice, finally speaking up.

He snorted back mucus, then shook his head.

Xander let out a breath, then placed a hand on Tommy's shoulder. "It'll be okay, you know," he said sympathetically, glancing at the thin cuts and knowing what the boy was feeling. The frustration of the pain, the added frustration of failing to release it. The thought that he couldn't even kill himself right. He'd felt it all many times in the past few months. Realized how many times after Sara died that he had been mean to Cathy, had taken it out on her... how he had been even worse than Tommy at times, many times, and still was even now. He sighed at his own stupidity while rubbing the boy's shoulder.

"It won't," Tommy sighed, shaking his head as more tears came down.

"Yeah it will. Believe me, man. I've been there."

Tommy looked up, meeting Xander's gaze for the first time since the whole thing started. "You?" he said, shock and awe in his voice.

For the first time, Xander noticed something in Tommy he never had - a twinge of jealousy, and envy. Not much, but enough. He smiled a little and hugged Tommy briefly, patting him on the back. "Yeah," he said softly, as Cathy moved in and joined in the embrace. "...me."

ᚑᚑ

Xander slammed the door to the car, pressing his head against the steering wheel in frustration. The horn beeped for a second from the impact, and he stared at its red imitation-leather center for a long moment, focusing in on every crack and indentation.

Cathy opened the passenger side door and slid in alongside him, leaning her head back on the rest and heaving hard. She turned to him, the light from the dash illuminating her pale face. "Do you think he's going to be okay?"

"He's talking to his Mother. That's all we can do."

She looked as though she were about to speak again, then nodded.

He chuckled softly to himself, a smirk growing over his lips.

Cathy turned on the headrest, looking at him with an odd expression on her face. "What's so funny?"

He sat up straight and turned toward her, running his fingers through his hair and then scratching the back of his head. "Given the choice between two murderers... I go after a suicidal, emotionally unstable teenage boy," he snorted, then laughed again, clenching his hand into a fist and slamming it against the dashboard, cracking it slightly with an audible -snap!-.

"You couldn't have known," she pleaded, touching his arm gently.

"Oh, yes I could have. I *wanted* it to be Tommy, and we both know it. I needed it to be him," he said, thumping his chest right over his heart once.

"Why?"

He paused as the gears turned inside his head. His eyes had a far off, distant look as things started to fall into place. "Because the alternative was too much for me to handle."

Xander reached into the back seat and grabbed his mother's cell phone, the one thing she insisted he bring with him if he took the car. Flipping it open, he dialed the number he'd come the have burned into his frontal lobe over the past few months, then pressed talk and brought it to his ear. Cathy just watched his mouth silently chanting the word 'please' over and over again.

"The cellular customer you have dialed is outside the service area, or has the phone turned off..."

"Ah!" he grunted angrily, snapping it shut again. "She never has her phone off."

Cathy nodded slowly, getting that same far-off gaze that he'd had a second ago. "Julie."

Xander just frowned at her as he dialed another number, nodding once curtly. "Julie." This time the phone rang.

After what seemed like an eternity, someone picked up. There was a moment's pause and then a hacking cough that made Xander yank the receiver away from his ear. "He 'lo?" came the tired-sounding voice on the other line, her voice slurred and sloppy.

"Miss Peterson?" Xander asked, pressing a finger against his free ear to hear better as static clogged the connection. "Dee? Is Julie at home?"

"Julie?" Dee responded, waking up a little, sniffing. "Haven't seen her all week. Came by and dropped off her bag, left again."

Xander sighed and closed the phone, not wanting to continue the conversation further. "Julie hasn't been staying there," he said to Cathy, tossing the cell back on the seat and turning the key in the ignition. "Hasn't been there in days."

Cathy sighed, rubbing one temple at the spot that Xander had once classified as the 'Peterson Syndrome' headache. "So we're looking at Julie?"

"'Death will keep following you, wherever you go, and I can't be a part of that anymore,'" he quoted as he pulled out onto the street, the entire car jolting with the sudden burst of acceleration as he sped down the street. "She wants death out of her life... no better way than to kill the killers."

"Where are we going?" Cathy almost screamed, gripping the handle on the car door and tightening her safety belt.

"Coral Cove," he growled, gripping the wheel. "There are some things you can only talk about with an ex."

𝄂〈〉𝄂

The room was mostly blackened by shadows, so much so that one could barely see the walls to get a grip on its size. In reality, it was massive. An abandoned poultry farm from Coral Beach's more industrious days. Sometimes you could still smell the hen droppings, if one tried hard enough.

There was one light hanging from a beam in the very center of the room, its metal shade ensuring that it shone on no more than a small circle.

Under the light, four men stood in a square, each looking more solemn than the next.

Ian Char's devilish grin was gone now. His face was panicked and sweaty, with two perpendicular scars down the right side of his face, a remnant of his last duel with the Black Womb. He was wearing tight jeans and a muscle shirt, not overly appropriate for that particular time of year, made obvious by the chill-induced goosebumps covering his arms.

Duncan Combs was silent and had a face like a statue. He just watched the rest of them, his icy stare moving from one to the next.

George McGyver stood tall; his posture perfect. His broad chest made him look strong for a man pushing sixty and his greying hair was combed neatly at all times. He might have been intimidating, if not for worried look his eyes gave as they darted back and forth in the darkness, as if petrified of its black.

Finally there was Quinton Travers. A fat, older man who was one of the people who'd been in the gang the longest. He had a laugh like a rabid hyena when he used it, but that time wasn't now. Now, he was deadly serious as he regarded the other three, stepping forward.

"Roulette is dead," he said simply, and they all hung their heads for a moment.

George reached up and touched his right shoulder, where his Tee tattoo had been placed years ago by Owchar, feeling the pull of sadness at his heart.

Travers paused, letting the words sink in. "So are at least thirty of our number, maybe more. It's not always easy to contact non-active members... not anymore. But we're trying. The police are trying to keep it quiet, but this is nothing short of an attack on our way of life. With Roulette gone, I'm taking control of our group. At least until we destroy whatever's doing this."

Ian's head shot up and he pushed the words through clenched teeth. "The Womb?"

Travers frowned. "I don't think so. He could have killed each of us so many times now and didn't... why all of a sudden, like this? It isn't his style. He likes to play the hero."

"Could be the Snakes," Duncan added, staring at a spot on the floor, his voice low. "With all that's been happening, they might think it's a good time for a power struggle. A lot of ex-Snakes are cops."

Travers nodded. "Maybe," he conceded. "But I think we're dealing with the Omegas. I think they're finally stepping up to the plate after that whole business a few months ago, right before the Womb started dogging us."

"What are we gonna do?" Ian asked, smirking a little.

Travers reached into the seat of his pants and produced a handgun. He cocked it once, letting the slide snap into place.

"We go to war."

Mike burst in through the front door of the Smith home, wood splintering around the deadbolt as he did so and flying out in all directions. The door swung hard, hitting the adjacent wall with a thud that echoed off of the walls of the house, reverberating back at him from every direction. Small fragments of wood sprinkled the floor in a semi-circle from the door, bouncing off of the carpet like confetti. He quickly looked around, hot sweat making his hair stick to his brow as he frankly searched for what he sought.

The door had opened directly into the living room, where a solitary sofa and ratted coffee table were all that kept it from being completely vacant. There was a pile of dirty magazines against a space heater near the sofa as well, and he could smell the distinct aroma of dust inside those heaters. Straight ahead was the entrance into the kitchen, where only a chair and part of the table were visible. To his right were the stairs, going both up and down, with extensions of the wall covering most of them, making it impossible to see the next floor without being on them.

"Mr. Smith?" Mike called out, blinking twice to adjust to the low light in the room. The muscles in his neck tightened as he clenched his fists and became stiff. He took an uncertain step forward out of the doorway, checking behind him only briefly to make sure there was nobody there. His eyes darted around the room feverishly, looking for anything that might be used as a weapon, or any spot where someone might be lying in wait. "Mr. Smith, are you home?"

There was no response.

Swallowing back hard, he took another step forward, then another, heading toward the kitchen. He had no desire to go upstairs or down to floors where no exit was readily available until he was absolutely sure he had to.

He stepped into the kitchen and felt the tile giving just a little beneath the weight of his boot. He realized he was tracking in snow and water, and briefly considered taking off his shoes, then thought better of it.

Unlike the front room, everything here was white and clean. The dishes were carefully put away, chairs neatly positioned at equal points around the table. On the table was a jar of pickles, a ketchup bottle, a loaf of bread, a two liter of Pepsi, carrots, and a head of lettuce.

Mike squinted at the arrangement, trying to determine what could possibly be made from the accumulated items. He took a step toward it, old floor boards creaking beneath him. His toe hit something under the table, propped up against the leg of one of the chairs, and knocked it over with a clang that made him jump.

Taking a deep breath, he knelt down to pick up the item. It was a metal grate, cut into even squares over and over again, and white except for a few twinges of rust where it had obviously sat for a long period of time

Standing again to examine it in the light, he recognized it as a shelf from a fridge.

Looking up and actually bringing the fridge into focus, he realized what could be made from the items assorted on the table: Room.

Letting out a sigh, he laid the grate onto the table and walked toward the refrigerator. He put a hand on the cold handle, pausing briefly, hoping he wouldn't find what he thought he would. Summoning his reserve courage, Mike opened the door wide.

His face turned white. Staring back at him with wide, open eyes was Don Smith. The eyes were fogged now, taking on a glassy, china-doll eeriness. His mouth was agape, several teeth conspicuously absent as blood dripped from it onto his naked body. Flesh had been torn away from his chest, ripped open like a suit, revealing the muscle and tendons beneath, stiff from the cold and exposure, but still moist with blood. His fingerless hands hung limply at his sides, caked in blood. His legs and arms were covered with cuts and bruises, many of them without visible surface trails of blood... they had been done after Don's heart stopped beating. His genitals were missing, replaced instead with a gaping maw... a crater that looked like it might have been created by a shotgun at close range. The man's face stared out at Mike, frozen in a scream that told all of his last horrible moments of life.

"Hey," came a voice from behind Mike, and he spun around in shock.

Derek Smith stood in the doorway of the kitchen, blocking the only exit from the room. His face and hair were spattered in blood, as was the knife that he held loosely by his side.

"I was saving that."

CHAPTER NINE
STRANGE

Reverend Gallagher sat in his office. The door was open, swaying back and forth slightly in the wind. The old hinges bayed mournfully each time their rusty joints were forced to move. The room itself was small and cluttered, filled with books and notes, and a bookcase full of diaries that he'd kept for years -- carrying them with him from one town to the next. The first Bible he'd ever gotten (a red-leather New Testament, given to him by his Godmother when he was confirmed) sat mounted like a trophy atop the case, its edges worn and the spine creased. On the walls were pictures of his mother and father, one oil painting of Jesus that had been in this office longer than he had, and many drawings and finger paintings given to him by the children in the Sunday-school classes over the years. There was also a simple wooden cross, splinters forming at the edges of it, held up by a nail is its apex.

The Reverend stared up from the growing pile of paperwork to gaze upon the cross, and the shadow it cast almost to the baseboards. He took a deep breath, shoulders rising, and then let out a heavy sigh.

The last file was of a mentally challenged girl named August Styles who had seen a steady decline in focus and willingness to cooperate of late. He closed the case file in front of him and then put it on a small pile on the floor. He frowned at the pile, only a few folders high yet he'd been at this for hours. He turned to the stack before him, at least three times that height, and he hadn't even taken all of the files from his office at the school. Even though Principal Shnieder had told him that he was free to use the office on school premises for as late as he needed, he was more comfortable here. This place felt like home.

Gallagher reached over to the next file folder atop the pile, a young man named Chesley Norman. He stopped, his fingers resting against the smooth, yellow surface of the folder. His thumb perused down through the rest of them, bending their edges up so that he could see the names of his students slowly flick by: Calla McFadden, Darrel Page, Karen Bennet, Cathy Kennessy, Alexander Drew.

He stopped, staring at that file for a moment.

He recalled once, months ago, when Alexander had come to him seeking solace after the death of one of his friends. Many of his friends, really, but one in particular. That had been at the beginning of all this madness, when the first wave of murders had happened, and he had thought that his flock would take forever to recover from the wounds. In truth, it hadn't taken that long, because more and more just kept coming, over and over again. And now, once again, they were in the same place.

He wondered how young Mr. Drew was handling it this time.

He let the pile go, picking up the file on Chesley Norman and opening it. She was a straight-A student, interest in technology...

He reached for his coffee mug (which read 'On the Eighth day, God created coffee... and it was good') and brought it to his lips, frowning when he found it to be empty. Sighing once again, he got up and walked over to his instant percolator, sliding the cup into its place and flipping the switch on its side. The light on the top of the ingenious device came on, and the water inside started to boil.

He turned as he waited for it to be finished, holding Norman's file before him, flicking down through the family history. The door squealed again, and he looked up at it. Just outside, he could see his confessional, looming ominously.

His brow furrowed as he looked at it, focusing hard. Something was wrong, and he couldn't put his finger on exactly what. Something was different, something small... but it tickled at the back of his brain nonetheless.

As he continued to stare at it, his focus changed suddenly, concentrating instead on the window beyond the confession box. His eyes became wide and his face pale as Chesley Norman's file dropped to the floor. "Lord Almighty!" he cried, backing up a pace and bumping into the shelf, jittering the coffee mug and causing it to fall from its perch, sending steaming hot coffee everywhere before shattering against the floor.

As the pieces of the mug danced and bounced about, one chunk stared upward, casting a shadow as long as the cross had a moment ago.

It said: God

CHAPTER TEN
CASUALTIES

"Derek..." Mike said softly, holding out his hand carefully, palm out, trying to appear calm, not wanting to get the killer excited. His eyes kept darting, almost uncontrollably, from Smith's small, beady eyes, to the knife that he gripped tightly between narrow fingers -- gripped so hard that he veins were popping out of his arms. "...How bout we put that down and talk?"

Derek smirked with the same cocky grin that had won him affection of the female variety right up through school. It smacked of confidence and self-assurance. His eyes squinted at Mike, the way they did at almost everything, seeming permanently narrowed. He licked his lips quickly, then spoke. "Or, I could keep this, and we could talk," he reasoned, his voice harsh yet full of lividity, as if he found the situation darkly humourous.

"Okay!" Mike spat out, just a little too quickly. "Okay, let's just talk then, man. We always used to talk..."

"Yes..." he laughed and took a casual step forward. Mike fought the urge not to take a step back and keep the distance between them. "...let's talk. 'Cause out of all the little fish swimming around this town, I think you were always the smartest one. Even smarter than me, most of the time."

"Thanks," he accepted, voice wavering.

"No problem," he chuckled, spinning the red-tainted blade between his fingertips. His square jaw moved from side to side, popping the bone within one of the joints to relieve some pressure. Mike's eyes wandered over him now, noting the blood covering his hands and arms... his clothes were clean, not even a spot on the white shirt that used to fit him perfectly, but was now stretched over large chest muscles. He'd been working out. And he must have changed his clothes after what he'd done to Don.

"You knew to come here. To you it was obvious. 'Go to his home.' Everyone else is out searching the woods, even after I gave them a clue..."

"The reason."

"Like that, did you?" Derek laughed, throwing back his head and opening his mouth wide, revealing blood-stained teeth. "I did that for you. I figured you'd want to be the one to play this hand of the game."

"The reason you killed to begin with, to help your father get ahead. To try and give him a story he could write about, win the Pulitzer prize and become famous, so that he might be able to spend some more time with you, instead of at work."

"Oo, good guess, but there is *another* reason..." he trailed and tossed the knife from hand to hand before it tight again. "And I kinda liked the song. You know, 'The Reason'? I think it kinda applies to this situation."

Mike was silent, his jaw set.

"Oh, you know the one... the one where the guy apologizes for all those things he did, says he's not a perfect person... and then just has one last thing he needs to do. Before he goes... Come on, Mikey, you know the words."

"Yeah," Mike nodded, forcing a smile.

"Tisk, man," Derek chided, bringing up his free hand and waving a finger back and forth scoldingly. "You're not speaking your mind here, buddy. Haven't we known each other long enough that you can tell ol' Derek how you feel?"

If I try to be nice, he'll know I'm lying and he'll snap anyway... Mike thought, mulling his words over in his mind. "I think you're ill, Derek. I think you need to get help, and I don't think they were giving it to you in jail. I think they were content to just lock you up and throw away the key, and that's not right."

Derek paused then tilted his head to one side to regard his friend. "That's the truth, isn't it?" he asked rhetorically. "Wow. Just when I think I know you... you throw me for a king-sized loop."

"Didn't see the point in lying to someone who's smart enough to know what I was thinking anyway," he said, again forcing his mouth into a lop-sided smile and hoping that Derek was ignoring the fear sweat that was pouring off of him now.

"Good boy," Derek mused. "I was going to kill you when I heard you down here... but you may just be fun enough to keep around after all. Nothing like that trigger-happy bitch of yours."

Mike clenched his teeth, resisting the urge to cry out in

response, to play right into Derek's hands. "Pfft. We're not even together anymore. She went south and dug Xander after she and he attacked you months ago. You can take her, but lemme tell ya, that's one ride that isn't worth the price of admission."

Derek paused, and then smiled a little wider. "Nice try. Didn't you just finish telling me that I knew a lie when I heard it?"

Mike swallowed hard.

"Just for that, I think I'll pay that price of admission before I go. She always had a thing for me anyway. Besides, you've got bigger things to worry about."

Mike's brow furrowed, his entire body clenching. "Like what?"

"Like what's really out there. Like who killed Owchar and the others. The Scooby Gang is about to head into the big leagues, Mikey."

"You... know?" Mike said, and even as he did, the realization was spreading over himself as well.

"Me and Julie always were such good friends... had so much in common... maybe I'll pay her a visit..." Derek mumbled, almost nonchalantly, as he brought the knife up to bear. "... Right after I'm done with you."

Derek leaped forward, crossing the distance between the two of them in two mighty strides. In flight, he tightened his grip on the blade, his thumb riding its edge. His eyes seemed alive, sparkling and glistening, mouth open wide and salivating as he thrust the knife forward.

Mike's eyes went wide, and he brought up both his hands to block the blow. He yowled as the sharp metal edge dug against the back of his arm near the elbow.

"Well, that was dumb," Derek laughed as he drew the blade back again.

Mike lashed out and slammed the base of his arm against Derek's side, knocking the wind out of him. The killer stumbled as air forced itself from between parched, cracked lips. Not wasting the moment, Mike football-tackled his opponent, sending the both of them sprawling against the kitchen floor. He drew back and struck quickly, slamming a fist against Derek's face, hearing the gratifying crack of a cheekbone as he did. Holding the man-monster's arm down with one hand, he pried the knife from his fingers with the other.

Derek shot his left knee up quickly, connecting with Mike's groin.

"Oh!" Mike bellowed, but did not let go of the knife and instead tightened his grip. He got up quickly so as to recover while Derek scrambled to his feet. Mike felt something sticky covering the rubber handle of the blade, and realized that it was blood. Don's blood. His mouth distorted from sickness and he watched as Derek steadied himself against the kitchen table, smirking as he wiped blood from his mouth as even more came out. Feeling the rage of the last few minutes build up inside him, he brought the blade up high then bellowed and lunged at Derek.

Derek moved to one side quickly and managed to intercept his foe's down-swinging arm. He forced it to continue the motion, lodging the blade into Mike's own leg.

Mike fell to the floor in agony as the blood rushed, pumping out with each beat of his speeding heart and sick from the overload of adrenaline.

"Heeeha," Derek laughed and slowly wrapped his fingers around the knife's handle, then yanked it out violently. He kneeled on the floor and grabbed Mike by the collar, forcing him to eye-level. For a moment, he just stared and smiled at his friend.

"I'm going to miss our talks." Derek plunged the blade deep into Mike's side. The bloodied teen's eyes bulged as he fell forward, only to be shoved back. His head knocked first against the table and then the floor. Derek withdrew the blade, paused and watched Mike tremble, then pushed it in again. He smirked with delight as the torso's tender flesh parted way to make room for the metal, again and again.

The third time he left the blade and rose slowly to his feet, never taking his eyes off of the body of Michael Harris and the blood that slowly expanding into an uneven puddle around him. After a moment, he turned and grabbed his black plastic jacket off of the couch as he headed toward the door.

"And Cain slew Abel..."

ᛉ

Warden Greyson turned his flashlight around, watching as the light bouncing eerily off of the snow-covered trees back at him. Although the night was cold, he couldn't help feeling hot underneath his uniform. He did his best to ignore the scent dogs barking all around him, each held back by a fellow officer searching for Smith, trying to pick up some sign of the murderer.

He breathed hard, each exhale sending a puff of crisp air from his lips. He watched it travel upward, then dissipate in the moonlight like smoke.

One of his men ran past him, the disappeared quickly into the foliage as if he had never been there. Although Greyson could hear him only scant meters ahead, the officer had vanished from sight.

He let out a sigh, even as he heard another come up behind him slowly. "It's hopeless. This place is like a maze, Davis," he said, his voice full of defeat.

Behind him, Davis heaved a heavy breath as well. "Smith stayed hidden for weeks, right under Tim White's nose. He's had months to think about this. We won't find him, sir."

"We have to keep looking. While there's snow on the ground, he can't keep his trail hidden," he said with confidence, turning the beam of his light to the right. Although buried under a snowy layer, he thought he noticed a patch that seemed disrupted and misplaced. He raised an eyebrow and called out to Davis, who'd moved on to the left. "Has one of the men been this way?"

Davis turned, counted the different flashlights and did some quick math in his head. "No, sir. Nobody's been down there."

Greyson turned, readied both gun and flashlight, then inched closer to the brush beyond the displaced snow.

"Now, I've got you."

He stepped forward slowly, circling around a large tree, keeping his light fixed on the spot just beyond the brush...

... until it came into view.

"...my God..."

CHAPTER ELEVEN
WAR GAMES

Xander gripped the steering wheel, feeling its texture give way beneath his warm touch. Cathy gripped her armrest as trees sped by at a blur. The only thing in steady focus was the full moon off in the distance, so far away it seemed to follow them across the highway.

"Will you slow down?" she squealed as the car fishtailed slightly on the slippery, slush-covered roads before righting itself. They passed a sign that indicated Coral Cove was some distance ahead, but zipped by it too quickly for her to see how far. "Do you want us to die before we ever even get there?"

"Please," he scoffed, his face twitching upward into a scowl.

"Fine, right. You've got a healing factor, I get it. That won't save me from cracking my head open against the pavement!" she huffed angrily, digging her nails into the upholstery as her eyes began to sting. She struggled to find something to focus on; to take her attention away from the high speeds while her stomach did back-flips inside her gut. As they went over a small hill, the vehicle became weightless for an instant and Cathy began to feel light-headed.

"How much further?" she managed to spit out, closing her eyes as the feeling subsided.

"One-point-nine-eight miles," he said matter-of-factly, cutting the wheel hard to get around a sharp turn, thrusting Cathy about in her seat.

She made a low, frustrated noise, but he did not tear his eyes from the road to see the expression on her face. He knew it too well by this time anyway. She closed her eyes and took a deep breath, steadying herself in the passenger's seat. When she reached some level of relaxation, she opened them again. "What are we going to do when we get there, anyway?" she asked, trying to find steadiness in her voice. "If she hasn't been with Dee, she could be anywhere, Xander. Coral Cove is a small town, but it's big if you have to go door to door."

He didn't say a word. Didn't even move except for his hands sliding over the wheel, navigating the meandering highway.

"That's assuming she's even in a house; that she's even in Coral Cove... she could be back home right now, if she's the killer."

Again, nothing.

She ran all of her fingers through her hair, stretching the skin of her scalp so much that her eyes widened against her will, then dug her nails in and ruffled her own hair just so that she could fix it again. She glanced briefly at her reflection in the side-view mirror. "Are you going to say anything, or am I just talking to myself? A few minutes ago, you couldn't decide which plan to follow through on, and now you've got none. Meanwhile, Mike's still back in Coral Beach, and he has no idea what's happening. This isn't smart, Xander--"

"It's Julie," he stated finally, turning to glance at her briefly. The moment that their eyes locked seemed frozen in time. It wasn't even a second, but it lasted so much longer. She watched the pain, anger and frustration swirl about in his pupils, like all the colors of pain mixing together, to form a look on the verge of tears.

"I know," she said softly. "But we still have to know how to find her."

"I can find her," he responded, as the first few houses started to whiz by. He let his left hand slide from the wheel onto the automated controls at his side, lowering his window and letting the cold winter air billow in. "All I have to do is get close to her."

Cathy's skin covered itself in gooseflesh, and a shiver crept its way up from the base of her spine into her shoulders, head and back down each arm.

Xander looked over at her involuntary movement and frowned softly. He took one hand off the wheel and placed it on her knee, squeezing it lovingly. She resisted the urge to bite her bottom lip as she placed her hand over his.

"I'm glad you're here," he said honestly, as he refocused on the road ahead. "I'm glad it's you. If it was anyone else, I'd be worse. And even though it's Julie... in some strange way, it feels right. It feels like if this is the end, it has to be the end of she and I as well... so that I can really move on."

Cathy nodded slightly, gazing upon his face from the

side. At that moment, she felt in tune with his thoughts. She knew each word before it came and could almost mouth along with his lips.

"Me too," she whispered. "I'm glad, now, that we can finally--"

She was cut off as she car screeched to a sudden halt, slamming the both of them forward against their seatbelts. The car spun to one side until it faced the woods on the side of the road evenly, displacing everything in the back seat. "Ah!" she hissed, as the seatbelt loosened itself once they'd stopped, revealing just how much it had dug into their skin.

Xander quickly removed his own before opening the door to the car and stepping out onto the road, heedless of oncoming traffic; just standing there on the pavement and snow with his arms stretched downward.

Cathy took off her own belt, letting it snap back against the wall of the car as the winch tightened. After waiting a moment for a car to pass by them, she stepped out and slammed the door behind her. She turned to face him, the car between them and yelled, "Have you gone ultimate bat-shit crazy?" Slamming a hand against the hood for effect, "You could have just killed us both, you fucking madman!"

His back turned to her; he curled all but the index finger of his right hand back into his palm, silently mumming her before taking a deep breath through the nose.

"What in God's name are you doing, anyway?" she asked, her voice calmer, but still audibly frustrated. As she spoke, she twisted her shoulder about to see if it was even still in its socket.

"I've got her scent, I just need to lock onto it," he said simply, taking another sniff.

She raised an eyebrow. "You can do that? From, like, anywhere?"

"Not with everyone," he said, eyes still closed. "But I know her scent. Know the aromas her body produces that she's not even aware of. I've spent the last week trying to get them off of me, showering day in and day out, smoking menthol, wearing cologne, hair spray... it's clinging to me. So it's not difficult for me to pick it up now."

"Huh," she said, tilting her head back a little. "Can you do that with me?"

His eyes opened wide and he spun around, much of the stiffness leaving him as he once again entered the car and put on his seatbelt. "Got her."

Realizing that he wasn't going to wait, Cathy scrambled in as well. Her feet were barely off the ground when he slammed his foot down on the pedal and the wheels screamed to life.

Julie Peterson brushed back a strand of her auburn hair, smiling devilishly as she braced herself against the kitchen counter. There was a mischievousness in her eyes as she opened the cutlery drawer, her long fingers dancing over the array of knives within. They settled finally on a long, slender blade with a black handle, clean and glistening in the light of the ceiling's fixtureless bulb that swayed slightly in the wafting breeze.

She smiled, biting her lower lip as she felt it between her fingertips, the soft rubber giving way a little from the heat of moist palms. Her freckled cheeks curled up as her grin grew wider still. She gripped the blade, turning toward the living room, where someone lay motionless against the couch, his head tilted back in an odd, obtuse manner, moaning.

She laughed a little, taking a step forward.

-SLAM!-

The front door to the house burst open, slamming again when it hit the adjacent closet door.

"Or, we could do it that way," Cathy sighed from a few steps behind Xander as he stepped in menacingly, both fists clenched at his sides.

"This ends," he said simply, his voice a deep, guttural sound. His voice box continued to reverberate even after the words were gone, emanating a low growl.

"Alex!" Julie yelped, jumping back a pace and nearly dropping the blade but instead clenched it tighter.

"You could have knocked. And there is a doorbell, you know," Cathy chided, folding her arms across her chest as she took her place at Xander's side.

"Hello, Julie," she said coldly, finally regarding the girl, looking her up and down. She was wearing a light blue terrycloth robe tied off at the waist, and there were purple pajama bottoms sticking out from beneath them. The edges and sleeves of the robe were worn and there was a conspicuous red stain traveling up one of the arms.

"What are you two doing here?" Julie yelled, her eyes going from shocked to angered. Her brow lines moved down and crunched in the middle, like two fault lines coming together to make a mountain. She tilted and glared specifically at Xander. "What are you doing here?"

"Don't play dumb," he spat accusingly, taking one menacing step into the house and pointing at her. "You don't need to, if you thought you were going to get away with this... you haven't been home all week. You went there and dropped off your bags and left again."

"You've been keeping tabs on me?" Julie screamed, tossing the knife down on the table so hard that it skidded and fell off the other side. "What the hell is the matter with you? Give up the hero bit for a stalker role much?"

Xander narrowed his eyes and slightly shook his head. "Don't play the innocent role with me. I know you too well, Julie."

Her eyes darted to one side and she looked downward. Cathy noticed it too, taking a step forward to remain at Xander's side, but keeping silent.

"What's in the living room that you don't want me to see, huh Jules?" he poised, almost laughing at his ex's indignance.

"That would be me," came a deep voice, followed by its shirtless speaker. He stepped out from around the corner before leaning against it casually. He wasn't overly toned, but he was shaped as though he might be one day. He was older than all of them and there was even the slight indication of greying hair scattered throughout the beard that covered his square, chiseled jaw quite evenly. His hair was short, black and curly, and more than a little bit messed up in the front. He glared at Xander with large brown eyes, that although angered, regarded the boy with an air of humor. "This is your ex, I take it?" he asked Julie, without once looking at her.

Julie looked at the floor, then back up again, blushing

a little. "Go wait in the living room, Jason," she said, turning back toward Xander. "I can handle this."

Cathy licked her lips, took a step back behind Xander and pretended that she had never been there to begin with.

Xander clicked his tongue against the roof of his mouth and blinked twice, but kept the line of sight between the two of them.

Julie's face was becoming even more red now, not with embarrassment, but with rage. "How dare you?" she grunted, her cheeks shaking.

He didn't say anything. He didn't move.

"What in God's name is the matter with you, Alex? God, why can't you just leave me the fuck *alone*?"

Xander's mouth twitched, and each of her words felt like it strapped another weight to his heart. "You've been here these last few days, haven't you?" he said quietly, feeling terribly ashamed, the feet which had been so well planted a moment ago now scuffing aimlessly along the floor. He took in a breath of air that confirmed what she was about to say even before she did. Her scent was everywhere, against everything... along with the stench of weed and beer and cigarettes. All three were also on her breath.

"Not that it's any of your business, but yes."

Xander's hand loosened, and Cathy stepped out from behind him, taking it, trying to give him some level of support. "Julie, listen..." she started.

"Don't," Julie spat, her eyes narrowing at her intruders' intertwined hands. "Where's Mike, anyway? Shouldn't he be here too?"

The both of them looked downward.

"Gotcha," she laughed. "I don't think either of you are in a position to call me any names right about now." She turned, honing in on Cathy. "At least when I was with him, I could keep him under my thumb."

The words hit them both straight in the gut, and her hand slipped away from his.

Xander looked up, seeing the cake on the table behind Julie for the first time now. "Julie, I'm--"

"Just get out," she snapped, waving him away in a final act of dismissal. She turned her back to him and leaning against the table.

He frowned, then turned toward the door. He lightly grabbed hold of the knob as Cathy walked ahead of past and out of the house.

"Xander?" Julie called as he was closing the door.

He didn't turn. He didn't need to to hear her robe falling to the floor as the couch springs expanded.

"He likes it when I surprise him in his room wearing next to nothing."

He did not make a single sound. He merely closed the door and walked back to the car where Cathy was waiting.

CHAPTER TWELVE
NEW RELIGION

Again Xander and Cathy passed a sign welcoming them to a town, but this time it was Coral Beach, and it was done at a much slower speed.

They had driven in silence ever since they'd left Jason's house with not even a stray look shared between them. Xander was driving casually with one hand now, his fingers loose, guiding the wheel with his palm. The momentum had gone from his thoughts, which now drifted in and out of one circumstance to another.

Cathy opened her mouth to speak, for at least the third time, then closed it again. She simply turned toward the window and looked down to watch the rocks and dirt fly past.

"Well, that was a waste of time," he said. The words were empty and hollow, and far too honest.

"We ruled her out," Cathy said matter-of-factly, her voice barely a whisper.

"Mm," Xander groaned. "We've ruled out all our suspects, Cat. The only person we know for certain did anything remotely close to wrong has had hours to hide, to run... or to kill half the population of the town, if he really set his mind to it."

"No road blocks," Cathy said pointedly, as they got closer and closer to town. "They either don't think Derek's going anywhere or they're very sure he's left."

Xander nodded, accepting that piece of information. He was silent again for a moment before speaking again. "She calls me Alex."

Cathy frowned, sighing. "I know. It bugs you, doesn't it?"

There was a pause, as he mulled the question visibly. "It did, once," he said honestly, pressing lightly on the accelerator.

"Listen," she said. No longer plagued by images of her head splattering against the road, now that Xander was going at something resembling a normal speed, Cathy was able to keep her eyes on him. "About what Julie said... about us..."

"Would you turn on the radio, please?" he interrupted, as if she'd never spoken, but politely all the same. When she did not respond, he looked at her and smiled. "There must be a good song or two on."

She smiled, laughing a little. "On this station, I wouldn't bet on it. The DJ's taste in music is like a pop star's taste in husbands."

He raised an eyebrow, not quite understanding that particular pop-culture reference, and making a mental note to ask Mike about it later.

She turned on the dial, and it came on midway through a word, making it hard to tell exactly which song it was.

There was an acoustic guitar strumming along almost aimlessly, and every couple of beats there was a single piano note. It was clear that the song was ending, even the words were few and far between, and yet it lingered on. For the briefest of instants, Cathy closed her eyes and let the notes enter her and grow into something tangible within her mind. sparkling down over her like rainwater.

She opened her eyes and looked out as the last wisps of forest gave way to familiar houses and buildings that greeted her with memories.

It was years ago now, too many for her to be exactly sure when. Before she and Mike had become an item, before high school, she was almost certain. There was a waterfall somewhere just outside the boundaries of the city, not too far from where she now sat. She had walked all of the way there, the sun blazing down on her bare back, burning it for days. There had been a towel wrapped carelessly around her neck. She had been wearing an extremely loose t-shirt of her father's, one far too big for her, over a one-piece swimming suit and flip-flops.

She remembered the way the trees felt as she brushed past them one by one, their branches caressing her sweet skin, sharply at time, but always taking care not to harm her. The leaves were bright green by this time, and their smell made the city seem far and away. She hopped over a rock covered in moss and mushrooms, then stepped carefully down a steep slope made more difficult by her choice of footwear.

On the radio, another piano note rang out, softly traveling along the air.

She had then come to a slippery ledge, overgrown

with plant life that seemingly defied gravity as it grew down the slope. Some large fruit hung over the gorge by the thinnest of threads, but making no effort or strain of it. She leaned over it, letting a few small stones tumble downward, clacking off of the large, flat rocks below. There was the pool, just like Dawn had said. It was a great, circular deposit of water fed by a waterfall that started even higher than the ledge where she now knelt. It was so deep that in its middle it looked black.

She scurried down the side of the cliff, no longer noticing the awkwardness of the flip-flops, her heart pounding in her chest with excitement now.

When she got to the bottom, she stopped, taking a moment to observe the calm flatness of the water. Except where the falls hit it, of course. But even that created barely any ripples. It was like a painting and the artist had carelessly forgotten to add waves.

Slowly, she let the towel fall to the rocky shore, kicking off the sandals and letting her feet into the water without even testing it first. A chill ran up her, but she quickly got used to it; it even felt warm once she was chest-deep. She felt the ground in front of her would give way, and extended her right foot to test the ledge's depth. The water there was black, and she could feel no sign of bottom, just the swirling moss and weeds and one or two sticklebacks brushing past her, curious as to what the girl was doing here.

Closing her eyes and taking a deep breath, she leapt into the deep water, feeling it caress every part of her body as she moved down, down, down until pressure started to build in her lungs and ears. When the ache meant she could go no further, even though she had yet to touch the bottom, she opened her eyes. There was no light to see, but there were snippets of motion all around her, surrounding her... and she became a part of it, silent and forever, all knowing.

She started kicking her chubby legs, moving back up toward the surface with her hair swirling about her with every motion. When she broke the surface again, she was beneath the waterfall, its cool onslaught pressing down upon her. She found a gap in its flow quickly and took in air from it, then moved to let some of the water travel down her throat and over her hair, washing the dirt and muck out of it and back into the river.

The piano sounded one last time, ending the song.

"That was Forever and One-Eighth of a Day by my personal favorite, Nine Stops Ten. You should find this album. I myself own three of them. I'm Tara Sampson for WCBR1 radio, and this is your hourly news..."

Xander watched the road, squinting at something up ahead. Meanwhile, Cathy came out of her trance and turned toward the radio, waiting to hear any news of what had happened while they were in Coral Cove. She wondered briefly why her thoughts had brought her back to that place, one of the most peaceful memories she had.

"Tragedy has struck Coral Beach yet again. A search party for escaped convict Derek Smith located the bodies of 30 recently-reported missing persons."

"Thirty?!" Cathy exclaimed as her eyes went wide, turning to Xander for some direction on what to feel.

He did not even break his concentration from the road ahead, turning the wheel slightly to follow it.

"Police say that Smith is not a suspect in the latest murders, explaining the disappearances were reported days before his escape. Although names were not made available, sources tell us the victims were fellow convicts or linked to area crimes. Police urge residents to be on alert as the manhunt continues."

"Tees," Xander said simply, his face not changing expression for even an instant.

"We have to go, Xander!" Cathy bolted frantically, suddenly unable to sit still in her seat as a million thoughts bounced back and forth inside her head. "Mike could be out there somewhere, not to mention Derek! We can't just wait for this to..."

"Cathy," Xander interrupted calmly, not looking at her.

"The killer's done all of this, what if Mike found him? What if Mike found Derek? What if Derek and the killer met one another, what if they were working together all the time, plotting this whole thing so that Derek could escape..."

"Cathy," he repeated, cocking his head forward this time as he slowed the car down.

"What if they're planning something huge with the Circe or Engen or something like that, and we're all too busy to notice before it's too late."

"Cathy," he said, looking at her finally as the car eased to a stop. Red and blue rays of light flashed rhythmically all around them. "Look."

She took in her surroundings for the first time since she'd turned on the radio. There were police cars everywhere, parked so close together that even if the two of them had wanted to keep going, they would have had to find some other route to take.

The building they were piled around was so tall and massive that Xander and Cathy had to get out of the car just to see right to the top of its steeple, or even its large wooden doors.

It was the Apostle Church, est. 1952.

"Lord," Cathy said in a hushed voice, bringing her hand up to her face. "What's happened here?"

Xander did not answer, unless the grinding sound his teeth were making could be considered a response. He started walking toward the door, watching nothing but their heavy iron knockers as they seemed to get closer and closer to him. Cathy circled the car and followed him, hurrying to catch up and even then to simply keep pace with her suddenly driven friend.

He heard a sob to his left, and turned to see Reverend Gallagher holding onto the door of an ambulance for dear life, as though it were the only branch keeping him from being sucked down into a mighty whirlpool. Tears flowed freely down the old man's cheeks as fast as he could dab them away with a handkerchief. His moans were deep and mournful, and he did not even bother to look up and see the two teens watching over him.

Xander stepped inside cautiously, looking from one side of the old church to the other. Reverend Gallagher had walked up to an aged table set up near the back room and poured up two cups of coffee, motioning for Xander to sit down. Drew smirked at the old man. "Isn't this traditionally done at a confession booth?" he joked.

Gallagher's bushy grey eyebrows lifted. "You have sins to

confess?" he asked, almost shocked.

Xander smirked, "I'm not what you'd call a religious man."

"That's not what I asked."

Xander sat down, taking up his coffee cup in one hand and chancing a sip on the hot liquid. It burned his tongue, and he felt the Womb veer up to repair the damage instantly. His eyes darted around the church nervously, always coming back to the visage of the son of God upon the cross, hanging dead center in the archway. He could still feel the spikes in his wrists from his own crucifixion, and felt a new empathy for the man on that tilted x. He looked at the kind old Reverend, who was smiling back at him expectantly, patiently waiting for the young man to speak.

"I can see I'll have to start," Gallagher laughed. "Shouldn't you be in school?"

Xander smiled, but it was fake. The smile that you give to older people when they ask questions such as those. "Schools got too many memories. Those old walls talk, y'know?"

"Indeed." He motioned all around him. "As do these walls. Often, late at night, I can hear the echos of a thousand spirits," he paused, staring Xander in the eye. "Recently, the voices of the dead have gotten louder."

Xander looked down toward his feet. "Yes, they have." There was a pause then while they both sipped on their coffees. "I'm having... problems... telling my friends about the events of these past weeks." he admitted.

Gallagher nodded. "I take it you lost someone close to you."

"Yeah. You don't get much closer then... her."

He nodded again. "Find guidance in the Lord, my son. He

will help you."

Xander took a sip of his java. "I feel like the Lord had aban-doned me, Father. I feel like I'm alone."

"Have faith, my son," the man said, touching him on the hand. "The Lord exists in all things. You may not find him here, but rather in a person. A loved one."

Xander took a last sip of his coffee, then put it down onto the table. He got up and began to walk toward the door. "Thank you, Father," he said, distantly.

Xander clenched his hands into fists, walking past Gallagher toward the mighty door of the church. He stopped then, because nobody had stopped him yet.

"What's wrong?" Cathy asked, coming up from behind him, looking over her shoulder at Gallagher again, who still had not noticed them. "Xander, talk to me. What's happened here?"

He didn't speak, merely turned and saw where many of the policemen were. They were out back, at the graveyard.

He turned and walked, slower this time, Cathy easily keeping pace with him. She heard him swallow back a large gulp of fluid, and there was something to his gaze that told her that he had at least some idea of what they were going to find here. At least, more than she did.

Halfway up the hill, Xander turned and acknowledged something simply, closing his eyes and nodding respectfully, but did not pause or break his stride.

Cathy looked where he had. It was a grave, one with no headstone. She furrowed her brow, and then realized that, in the darkness, there were shards of where a headstone had been sticking up from the ground. Behind that were the shattered remains of it, turned mostly to dust and pebbles. She became confused, looking around for a moment to get her bearings, then realized whose grave it was.

It had belonged to Frederick Windsor, whom most people had called Sud. He'd been shot by the Tees while at school.

Her hand immediately came to her mouth as she gasped, tears welling up in her eyes. She turned away from the horrible sight, running to catch up with Xander, who was almost at the top of the hill.

"Xander!" she called, the salt water reaching her cheeks now, and then the snow and grass below.

He stopped, his face hanging downward.

She thought he was stopping to wait for her, but when she reached him, she realized he was again paying his respects. They were standing next to another shattered headstone, this one covered in flowers and cards and letters. This one she recognized instantly. She had not long ago written one of those letters, and some of the roses had been bought by she, Mike and Xander together, trying to give the grave some light in the bleak weather.

It was Amanda Peterson.

Xander continued without a word as Cathy fell to her knees, digging her hands into the snow and making them cold and blue. She reached out and grabbed a rose in the palm of her hand, squeezing until juice ran forth from it from between her fingers. Rose oil mixed with her tears and fell to the snow, staining it the same dark red as blood.

After a moment of fighting the heaving gasps that attacked her body now, she turned to Xander, wondering why she could not feel his comforting, warm touch on her somewhere.

When her eyes found him, she realized why.

"No..."

He stood at the top of the hill, which was covered completely in snow, many sets of tracks going to and from it, including his own. He was looking downward, his hands shaking and then becoming fists, clenching tighter and tighter until she saw tiny drops of blood slither down his palms and drip from his knuckles. All at once, he fell to his knees without warning, his upper body still perfectly straight and rigid, staring down at what lay before him.

Even though he had his back to her, she knew that he was crying.

He was standing at the grave of Sara Johnson.

Her lower lip quivering, Cathy rose to her feet and followed his footprints up, keeping her eyes glued to the snow. They caught a shard of granite as she got closer to him, followed by a mound of displaced dirt, frozen and crystalline. She swallowed hard as she came up behind him, seeing the headstone smashed into at least two dozen separate chunks, but that was not where he was looking.

And then she knew, just as he had from the start. And just like him, she could not believe it until she saw it for herself.

Xander bent over quickly, pressing his face into the snow, as the shake that had started in his fists now enveloped his entire body. When he moved, all at once she saw what she knew had been there all along.

Sara looked up at her with eyeless sockets, removed

from the ground from the waist up, a light layer of snow covering her body. Her skeleton showed through in places, but much of the skin of her face had remained, blue and pale and clinging to the bone with nothing but the fact that nothing had displaced it yet. The shoulder-length blonde hair that had once bounced and shook magically with her every movement was now longer, and it had taken on the appearance of dead hay, stiff and brittle. Her clothes were stained brown from the decay of her body and time spent in the ground, but it was still the white blouse and black satin dress that she had been put to rest in. Her mouth was closed, and for a moment, she almost looked as though she might wake up.

Xander reached out, carefully caressing her cheek with one finger, the flesh moving against his touch and never going back once it left, having long ago lost all its elasticity. "I'm sorry..." he mumbled between tears, almost inaudibly. Even Cathy hadn't really heard him, so much as she knew in her heart what he had said.

He let his hand trail down to her shoulder, grabbing it. As his head began to shake, not from side to side but rather vibrating in general along with the rest of his body, he pulled her carefully close to him, finally bringing her head to rest against his lap, stroking her hair, a great deal of which came out under the pressure.

"Xander..." Cathy said, soothingly, reaching out to touch him on the shoulder.

He thrust his head back, mouth open wide, and let out a long, deep bellow that echoed off the hills that were still miles away, clutching his dead lover close to his heart before collapsing onto it again.

Cathy returned her hand to her side, just watching her friend as he cried, knowing full well that that was all she could do right now.

"... Harris..."

She turned, seeing an officer standing a few meters down from them, smoking a cigarette and holding a cell phone to his ear. She squinted at him, as if focusing her eyes upon him would make her hear him better.

He turned in her direction suddenly, then dropped the smoke to the ground.

She took a step toward the Officer, again, knowing exactly what was about to happen, yet having to experience it to be sure.

When she got close enough that he could see who she was he turned away again, stepping to one side of his squad car.

She turned to one of the other officers. "Do you have a phone I could use?"

He eyed her suspiciously. His jaws seemed too large for the rest of his head.

"Please?"

He frowned, then took a small flip cell phone from his back pocket and handed it to her. She paused a moment, trying to remember Mike's number.

"Put it down."

"Excuse me?"

"You heard me, Xander Drew, put it down." Sara Johnson's voice echoed her own words. Her voice was like springtime. "Are you going to? Or are you going to make me repeat

myself again?"

Xander looked at her with surprise and puzzlement, and not for the first, or the last, time. "And again I say, excuse me?"

"You have been at those damn Chemistry books for ten hours straight. You need to relax, and something tells me that I'm just the person to help you." Her back was arched, making her even more sexy then Xander could've ever thought possible. She wore cut-off jeans, with a sleeveless tube top, a modified fish-net stocking providing a sleeve for one arm, which held a smouldering smoke in it. The summer sun beat against the back of her head, creating a halo effect around her hair. She looked like an angel.

"But Sara, I still have to go over the Bronsted-Lowry acid and base tables, and ... "

She smacked the books to the ground. "Give it up! Come outside. Have fun. For me?" When she said "For me," she gave him little puppy dog eyes. He loved that. He loved her. More than life.

"Let me get my coat," he sighed.

"Yah!" she chimed, walking in with him and waiting in the hall. She looked at him for a second. "I love you, Xander," she said suddenly, cheerfully.

He looked up from tying his sneakers and into her eyes. She was serious. "I love you, too."

Xander lay on the ground, broken and beaten by Julian Grendel, who was Sara's current boyfriend. Blood seeped from his upper lip, making the bottom of his face warm and wet.

"When are you going to stop doing this?" she had asked him, using his shirt to wipe a bit of the blood away.

He looked up at her, smiling. "I guess when I start winning fights."

"Not that," she giggled, wiping more blood from his forehead. "This. Chasing after every boy I go out with like some... jealous father."

"Oh," Xander said, looking downward. "I guess when you start going out with reasonable guys."

"What do you mean?"

"Gee, I wonder. Grendel, Derek, Sud, Tommy, Jamie, Travis, Cecil... the list goes on. Guys that are... okay, but they don't deserve you. You deserve someone special. Someone who'll treat you right and make you feel good and... and not look at you like you're an object. You're better then you think you are, y'know. You deserve better than you think you do."

She smiled, then leaned in and kissed him on the cheek. "That was the nicest thing anyone ever said to me. Make me a promise."

"Anything."

"Don't ever give up."

"Huh?"

"Don't ever stop protecting me. And when I finally do find that guy you were talking about, protect someone else. This world needs a protector, Xander."

"I promise."

"Don't ever give up"

ᗢᐩᗢ

"So, you going to Julian Grendel's party on Friday?" Sara asked him, paying little attention to his response or even if he gave one.

"Uh, I'm not sure. I was thinking about hitting the Factory with Mike," Xander replied, half concentrating on her and half watching out for Grendel himself.

"Oh, come on, Xander," she whined. She said his name like it was some kind of a joke.

"All right, I'll come. But you have to promise me you'll make sure Mike and Cathy don't ditch me like the last time," he reasoned, heaving a massive sigh as he gave in.

"They didn't ditch you."

He gave her a droll, tired look.

"They didn't!" she laughed, slapping his arm playfully.

He frowned, then rolled his eyes and nodded.

"Oh, come on. Don't sulk. You know I'm right. They love you."

"They do," he agreed finally. "They really do. They love me and they're there for me and they are the best of friends - except in public. In public, it's like we never met."

"Drama Queen."

"Oh, I'm not saying they try it or anything... it's just the way things are. I get it." He forced a smile, making eye contact with her. "I don't even think they realize they do it."

She gave him a little smile, the right corner of her lip curling just enough to make her irresistible as she fixed her black tube top, even though it hadn't really needed it.

"I promise," she said, after she had spent enough time fiddling with her attire to make him twitch. "They'll be good little boys and girls, as long as you are."

He snorted, rolled his eyes, and closed his locker door with a clang.

"So, what's new today?" he asked, shooting her a smile. "Anything scandalous going on?"

"Well," she started, smirking to herself proudly. "I heard from Julie Peterson today that the reason Derek has been so on edge lately is because Theresa had to take the test."

"Yeah," Xander nodded. "That Family Living test was bad news. I think I must have only gotten an eighty-five or something..."

She turned and gave him a little slap on the arm. "Not that test, you halfwit. A pregnancy test."

Xander's eyes went wide for a moment as he held open the front door for her, which she barely acknowledged. "Oh."

"Yeah."

"Why would Derek be messed up over that?" he asked naively.

She shot him a look.

"Ah. Forget I asked."

"Done."

"Wasn't she supposed to be with Jamie?"

"They broke up."

"Why? I mean, besides the 'she may be pregnant from another man' thing?"

"That's just a rumor. The real reason was because he cheated on her," she smirked to herself coyly.

"With who?" he moaned, feeling a relantionship headache coming on.

"Me," she said proudly, and he realized that this would become a migraine before it was over.

Xander finished walking home with Sara, like always. They lived next door to one another, and had since either of them could remember. Since they were children. Every day he'd remember little things like where he'd fallen out of the tree trying to sneak up to her room when they were six, when she had been sick and *wanted to play. Or on his lush, green lawn where she had found out how he felt when they were twelve.*

He had had a huge crush on her that summer and had been sitting on the sidewalk between their houses, burning their initials into a piece of wood. She had started toward him on roller blades and he had dropped the wood and ran into his house. She'd picked it up and looked at it, then thrown it into the trees on her way down the road, never actually speaking of it. He could still remember the scent of the wood as it burned every time he thought of it. It was the way love smelled.

At that age, most children were confident of their own immortality. That they could do anything, and go anywhere. But it was then that he realized how different he was from his friend. She was a princess in their school. Other kids wondered why she lowered herself to talking to him. He was . . . abnormal. Subnormal. Less than human. Those who actually took notice of him could barely stand him. But when he was around her, none of it mattered. On that ten minute walk from home to school and back again, the world could fall down around his ears and crush him every day, and he wouldn't care. He would ask for more.

She walked up her driveway and through the off-white door into her house.

He watched it for a second after she was gone as if she were still there, then walked into his own house.

"Enjoying the party?"

"Most definitely." Xander said enthusiastically.

She smiled at him.

He got lost in it for a moment, just staring at her. Her eyes were glossy, and he could see the brush strokes on her cheeks from where she had applied her makeup before going out.

She smiled at him again, nodding her head and waiting for him to speak.

"Oh!" he said finally, laughing humorlessly. "I had something I wanted to talk to you about."

"Okay," she chirped, still bobbing along to the song in her head. "Anything in particular?"

"Yes," he said. "No. Maybe."

"Glad we cleared that up."

"It's not any one thing. It's... look, we've know each other a long time, and --"

"Hey! You dropped one! You gotta take a shot!" she howled at someone from across the room, pointing at them wildly with her drink hand. She was still laughing when she turned back to him. "Sorry."

"That's okay."

"What were you saying?"

"Yes. What I was saying. What I was saying was -"

"This is the end of this year's flute hanger!" someone called from the next room.

Sara laughed, so hard that she almost fell over onto Xander.

"Hey, listen, you wanna go talk?" he asked, smiling as she helped herself back to her feet. "This place is a little loud."

"Yeah, sure."

He motioned toward the curtains he'd been playing with. When he pulled on the drawstring next to them, they opened and revealed a sliding glass door that lead out onto the balcony.

"Sly," she said, tossing him a playful wink. "If I didn't know better, I'd have thought you planned this."

Xander laughed.

The two of them walked out onto Grendel's balcony. The cool night air whipped at them, her light blonde hair blowing gracefully backward, exposing her neck and chest. He found himself looking at her unintentionally.

"Dear God you're beautiful," he said finally, with the honesty of a person who had been waiting forever to say it.

She smiled at him, with those beautiful lips that she had painted a sparkling platinum for the occasion. "Excuse me?"

"I said you're beautiful," he repeated, turning to look her square in the eye.

"Yeah." she laughed. "I got that. But why?"

"Because," he said, taking her hand. "You are."

He leaned in to kiss her. She looked up at him, moving in slightly herself, her lip quivering in an anticipation she hadn't even realized she had had until now. Her eyes fluttered back and forth between his lips to his eyes and his did the same, making eye contact every so often. He could smell her perfume and it overwhelmed him. He could feel the softness of her body, so close to his and yet still not touching. Slowly, they moved closer together. Closer...

"Xander," came a voice from inside.

"What?" Xander turned, angrily.

"We need you for something in here." It was Dave Marston, a jock friend of Jamie's. "It's this weird thing with Gren's computer. Some kinda net nanny keeping us off. You wanna...."

"Yeah. Just... gimmie a minute."

"All right."

Xander looked at Sara for a long moment, smiling. "Hold that thought."

If you're innocent, you're hurt, or you're scared... I'll be there.

"Xander, we have to go!" Cathy cried, more tears than she'd ever thought possible.

He had laid Sara back down now, and in fact was standing again, looking down at her upturned head. He did not respond to her, just stood where he was, seeming to be off in a daze.

"Xander, Mike's been hurt! The cops found him at Derek's and took him to the hospital! They're not sure if he's going to make it!"

"...gonna get them..."

"Yes! Agreed! We'll get Derek for this, and we'll get the murderer, and if someone different did this to Sara we'll get them too, and if we have time left over maybe we'll round up the Tees..." her entire face was red and puffy, and looked almost deformed with grief. "But right now, Mike needs me and I need to go to him and I need you to help me, Xander!" she wailed, curling her hands against her chest in some version of the fetal position.

"...Julie..."

Tears still coming, she furrowed her brow in absolute frustration, her mind unable to handle what he was saying at the moment. "What?"

"I'll kill them all," he said, his voice so low that it had moved past a growl and become almost like the harsh voice of the Black Womb.

"No..." she whispered, backing away from him a pace.

"Please, no..."

Blood started to gush from the wounds his fingers had made in his palms now, and she realized that he had popped his talons *after* he'd made his hands into fists. The redness seeped down onto Sara's rotting corpse, then turning slowly darker and darker until it was black.

"Tommy, Travers, Roulette, Derek, Julie, Raine, Black Heart, Zakron, Genblade..." he thrust his hands into the air, even as the Darkness flowed over them, meeting at the center of his torso and splashing outward, doubling the speed at which they covered his body. "They'll all pay! They will! I'll make them! You hear me? I made a vow on this woman's grave once before... that if you were innocent, you were hurt or you were scared... I'll be there! Well tonight, I make a new one!" he screamed, his entire body covered now as he screamed in rage and hate at the city below him.

"No..." Cathy sobbed, stepping back steadily now.

"Unless you're innocent, I'll be there! I'll make you hurt, make you scared! You're all guilty, and I'll have this town shake with fear!

"Black Womb lives!"

He cried, as the ooze covered his head, quickly forming three red slits, opening to form his eyes and mouth. He turned, his muscular form looking Cathy up and down, then with one great leap was at the bottom of the hill, and seconds later in the forest surrounding the graveyard.

"God, no..."

CHAPTER THIRTEEN

Mike lay on the stiff, metal bed of the operating table as a doctor finished sewing the last of his wounds shut.

"We've got some seepage over here," called a nurse.

The anaesthesiologist rushed to Mike's side as the monitor beside him began to beep and flash wildly.

Cathy buried her head in her hands as the cab sped ever closer to the hospital. It was easily going as fast now as Xander had been going down the highway earlier, but she did not notice this time.

She was all out of fear.

The Black Womb landed against a thick tree, burrowing its claws in deep as it slanted its red eyes, surveying the homes just beyond the brush and the people that walked the streets near them.

Reilly changed Mike's IV bag quickly, tossing the empty one aside. "His heart rate's fading..." she cautioned, keeping one eye on the monitor as she worked, her face a stone as more liquid ran into his veins.

"...I can't stop the bleeding..."

The Womb slammed Tommy against the wall of his bedroom, making him scream in terror and pain, unable to look away from the creature's glowing red pupils.

"Tell me!" it demanded, turning and tossing the boy against the far wall.

"I don't know!" Tommy cried, cradling his newly dislocated shoulder.

Mike's face twitched, looking pained as the doctor finished suturing a long gash near his leg. The numbers on the monitors still changed constantly, rising and then falling again before repeating the process. As he watched in horror, blood started to seep out into the table from a wound he'd thought was closed.

He pushed his way past Reilly and the anaesthesiologist, a panicked look coming over his face as he tried to deal with the new bleed. "I need some help here!"

Cathy threw a wad of bills at the cab driver, not even stopping to see if she'd paid enough or too much as she leapt from the cab. She took off running toward the re-volving doors of the hospital emergency entrance. Her eyes were bloodshot.

⋌⋎⋏

The Womb smashed through Derek's window, star-tling a police officer that was hunched over and pressing a cotton swab to a puddle of blood in the kitchen.

"What the fuck?!" he yelped, falling backward onto his ass and then fumbling for his gun.

The Womb lunged feet first at the cop, driving both its heels into his jaw. The officer went flying against the cupboards before he cracked his head and was knocked out cold.

The monster raised its nose high in the air even as it moved to the open fridge, sinking its claws deep into the back of Don Smith's cold shoulder and pulling him out. The body tumbled to the floor and the Womb peered in-side for any clue. It sucked back air and closed his eyes. When they opened, the light glistened off their cherry sur-faces, and it realized that the scent of Derek Smith had not been here in hours.

It bellowed.

⋌⋎⋏

Cathy pressed a hand against the glass door of the OR, watching as more and more people rushed in to help. Reilly left, urged once into the garbage can just outside the room, then continued down the hall.

Cathy turned and buried herself into Mike's father's shoulder.

ᐱᐱ

The surgeon heaved a sigh of relief as he closed the last of the wounds. Mike, still intubated, was wheeled out of the operating room into the recovery area.

ᐱᐱ

Black Womb jumped from the shadows of a bush, pressing his hands against the shoulders of a twenty-something man, forcing him onto the pavement.

"Where!?!" it bellowed, smelling the whiskey on the man's breath.

ᐱᐱ

Cathy sat next to Mike, her hand touching his, listening to the steady beat of his heart monitor. She was afraid to do anymore. Afraid she might somehow hurt him. She wanted to get closer, to let his hospital gown soak up her tears, but instead they fell to the floor in a rapidly expanding puddle.

ᐱᐱ

The Womb turned over Megan Greene's desk, sending her backward onto the floor. She raised a hand to defend herself, her eyes sparkling with horror between her shaking fingertips.

ᐱᐱ

Mike's eyes opened slowly, and he turned toward Cathy, smiling a little.

She laughed, the tears of sadness ending, replaced immediately by a different sort. "Hey," she said simply, her voice squeaky and uneven.

"Hey..." he tried to reply, then gagged, noticing the tube in his throat for the first time. He looked as though he was about the throw up, and the monitor next to his bed began to scream again.

Cathy got up and backed away from the bed, cupping her mouth with her hands as two nurses rushed back into the room.

A panicked, fearful look came over his face and he clutched at the tube and tried to pull it out, feeling as it slid along the inside of his throat, scratching and biting at it and his muscles tried to contract to stop it.

"No!" one of the nurses shouted, but he pulled away.

Cathy screamed.

⋏⋎⋏

The Tees turned as one, the smile fading from Travers' face as he swirled his gun around to point it at the doorway, which hung open awkwardly.

There was nothing there.

"What..." George mumbled, even as his question was answered in the form of a guttural hiss.

⋏⋎⋏

"Honey, you've got to lie down!" Cathy pled, placing her hands firmly against Mike's chest.

"No, Cathy! You don't understand! I know who the killer is! We have to stop him!"

All four men turned toward the center of the room, where the Black Womb sat crouched, its elbows resting against its knees. Swirls of aqua had appeared in the redness of its eyes and grown like whirlpools until there was nothing left but the blue-green tint.

"It's the Black Womb."

-Bang!- Ban-Bang!-

Quinton shot wildly, bursts of light predating each blast for a fraction of a second, illuminating the rest of the room like lightning. The Womb flipped aside, landing back against its toes and then using the momentum to spring forward.

"Black Womb lives!" it bellowed mid-air as Quinton fired twice more. The three others pulled their own pistols out from their jackets and Ian double-checked to make sure that his was loaded.

The creature ignored the shots, swiping out with its massive claws when it got close enough to Travers, not batting the gun away but instead stabbing its index claw right through the man's palm then pulling backward in one mighty stroke. The gun went in one direction, off into the darkness... the man's middle finger and a great deal of blood went in the other direction, spattering some of the red liquid against Duncan's face.

Quinton fell to the floor, clutching his disfigured hand

as blood spewed uncontrollably from it, some even going into his mouth as he cursed wildly.

All three of the others opened fire at once, six bullets finding their way into the Womb's chest and gut within seconds. It stumbled backward from the sheer force and its healing factor kicked into high gear. George watched in horror as the bullets squeezed their way out of the holes they'd created, rattling against the floor in the order they'd entered.

He changed his aim, firing up slightly.

The Womb's left eye seemed to explode in a splash of aqua and the creature screamed, bringing both its clawed hands up to it's face and only causing more damage.

"Yes!" Duncan cried, pumping his arm in the air while using the sleeve of the other to wipe Quinton's blood from his face.

"Keep firing, you idiots!" Travers belched out between gasps of pain.

The Womb looked up from his hands, its monstrous face expressionless, its eye back as though it had never been gone.

It swiped its claws down low, its arm seeming to extend as it did, like swinging an elastic with a weight on the end. They dug into George's ankle, shattering the bone and flipping him onto his back. With one massive leap it was on the man, who was now screaming almost in perfect tune with Travers. The demon dug its claws into the gang-lord's chest ripping downward. George brought the gun up point blank to the Womb's face, putting quick first pressure on the trigger.

The Womb opened its mouth as wide as it could, revealing duel rows of long, yellowed, jagged teeth. It shot its head forward, biting down on George's wrist even as the rapist's shot blew out the back of the Womb's skull.

The Womb, still holding George's hand and gun in its mouth, twisted its legs in a way no human and few animals could, propping them against George's chest and shoving backward into a back-flip that took him halfway across the room, taking George's hand with it.

The creature landed right next to Ian, spitting the now useless appendage out and slashing quickly under the man's arm and simply tossing his against a wall twenty feet away before he could even fire a shot.

It turned its focus to Duncan, whose gun was shaking and empty.

Growling darkly, it leaped.

𝄐〉𝄐

Cathy opened the door to the barn.

She gasped, closing her eyes.

Xander knelt naked in the center of the large storage room, the air thick with blood and gunpowder. All around him was a huge puddle of discarded black ooze, and his body was covered in a thin layer of congealed blood from head to toe, weighing his hair down tight against his scalp.

The only light was directly upon him like a spotlight, making it hard to see anything else until her eyes adjusted.

When they did, she saw the parts.

There was a hand in the corner.

A head with a large, animalistic bite mark taken out of

it lay not far from where they stood, a look of terror frozen onto its face, a horrifying tribute to Quinton Travers's last few moments of life.

Propped up against the wall closest to Xander was a naked body, fat and covered with hair, shards of his clothing scattered all around him, so weighted with blood they did not blow in the draft created by the open door. Cathy recognized it as George McGyver. He was missing a leg and both his arms... and his genitals.

Somewhere in the room, someone still breathed heavily, quick, small breaths. For a second, Cathy dared to hope that someone had survived... and then the breathing stopped, and there was the sound of something hitting the floor. She winced.

Xander turned toward her, tears rolling freely down his cheeks. He opened his mouth to speak but found that he could not. It hung there, open, waiting for words, the layer of blood stretching over it, which he made no effort to remove.

Slowly, Cathy stepped toward him.

She stood next to Xander and looked down at him. His eyes were still partially black.

All at once he moved forward, wrapping his arms around her legs and hugging his face into her mid-section, covering her lower half in blood.

And he wailed.

. . .

Xander sat on the corner of his bed, facing the wall but not quite looking in its direction. He gripped tightly onto his pillow and curled around it in the fetal position. He rocked mindlessly, back and forth, back and forth...

He'd hardly said a word since they brought him home from the warehouse. Cathy had helped him into shower, but she didn't think he had even been aware of it. He would periodically stop crying, sometimes for a full twenty minutes, then something would flip a switch inside his brain and he would start again. There were always more tears, and as Mike watched him start again, shoving his head into the pillow, he thought maybe the Womb regenerated, replenished his tear ducts, giving him more moisture to seep out.

He briefly thought of that as a good thing, then turned back to the tiny print of the file folder he cradled in his hand.

Cathy sat next to Xander, her index finger gently caressing the back of his hand in a fluid, repetitive motion, but achieving no response. It was as if she were touching fresh mortar, cold and wet. She turned from Xander's blank stare to the bandages revealed by Mike's open shirt, unable to find a sight that would allow her mind to rest.

Xander didn't seem to be breathing.

His eyes shot at her for a split second, then returned to their forward gaze at the screen saver bouncing around his screen, displaying the time, counting away the seconds.

Mike flipped back a page, scanning through the document that seemed to randomly change font and size, sometimes escaping into O'Toole's scrawled version of handwriting. "Got it," he said finally, but without satisfaction.

Cathy looked up, leaning forward just a little, but not taking her hand from Xander's. "Yeah?"

"What does it say?" Xander said haggardly, though his lips barely moved. The sound startled them both, as if they'd forgotten he was capable of it.

"It's that word again... amalgam. The one he kept repeating over and over. He finally decided to explain what he meant by it."

"And?" Cathy persuaded, coaxing her boyfriend to continue.

Mike scanned through the rest of the document, flipping over to read the first few lines of the next page, his eyes moving back and forth quickly. "Says he'd drugged you. He calls it an 'association-response chemical molecular adhesive.' Something the boys at Engen or Circe cooked up more than likely, though it doesn't say for sure. He used it on you during the hypnosis sessions... all of us for a while, until he started to narrow down exactly which one of us he was looking for."

"What did it do?" Cathy asked, hushed; she felt shocked and violated.

"Whatever he wanted it to. He'd introduce it before each session, then use the session to program that specific dosage. He really laid it on Xander though... keeps using the word 'amalgam'... and 'merge'... doesn't say how he administered it, though."

⋏⋎⋏

"So, how do we do this?" Xander asked, trying desperately not to make it sound like a groan.

O'Toole smiled at the young man's compliance, although it had to be forced out of him. He reached into the breast pocket of his faded blue shirt and pulled out a gold pocket watch. "I'll be placing you into a hypnotic state, Mr. Drew. While in that-- "

"With that?" Xander said, raising an eyebrow and pointing at the pocket watch, engraved, 'To Warren, for many years of loyal service.'

"Excuse me?" O'Toole stuttered, trying to find his words after being interrupted.

"You're seriously going to try and hypnotize me... with a pocket watch?" he laughed skeptically.

Warren smiled, dangling the golden circle confidently. "Why, yes, actually."

⋏⋎⋏

The younger man clicked his tongue against the roof of his mouth a couple of times, letting saliva slosh in and out of the gap in his two front teeth. "Can I see it first?"

O'Toole smiled wide, handing him the trinket.

Xander held it in the palm of his hand, watching as the lamp light from the Counselor's desk gleamed off of its gold plated surface. He bit his lip as he saw his own reflection in it, and could almost picture himself transforming. Could almost feel the beast inside of him breaking down barriers, clawing at the doors of Drew's consciousness, waiting, wanting. Wanting the blood. As he stared at the watch, O'Toole's heartbeat seemed to get louder and louder until it was all that Xander could hear; like a soft drink machine with 'drink me' scrawled across it.

"I'd like to have that back now." O'Toole coughed, reaching out and grabbing the clock by its chain. "Is there anything else before we begin?"

⋔

O'Toole cleaned his thick, round glasses, placing them back on his face. He grabbed his pocket watch from its perch, pinned to his lapel, and let it drop, dangling from its chain.

⋔

Warren picked up the watch by its chain, handing it to Xander, who watched it (as if already in a trance) for a moment as it spun in one direction, then another.

⋔

He cleaned the watch, making it gleam, then carefully placed it back in his breast pocket, careful not to smudge it again by touching it with his bare hand.

⋔

Xander held the watch, spinning it slightly between his thumb and forefinger.

⋏⟨⋏

"It was on the watch," Xander sighed, raising his head from the pillow, his eyes looking tired and old. "He never, ever touched it with his bare hand. And I always asked to see it before I went under, to touch it... he always pretended to resist. That lying..."

"That was probably one of the predominant suggestions he implanted," Mike nodded slowly, recalling his own experience with the watch, even though he himself had never actually gone under. "A desire to hold it whenever you saw it."

"What else did he get us to do?" Cathy almost whispered, shifting uncomfortably on the bed covers, imagining what such a drug could have gotten her to do without her even knowing about it.

Mike saw his lover's discomfort and quickly found her section of the passage. "Umm... not much for you, actually. He was getting you to repress bad memories, but there was also some kind of associative trigger on them. He was locking things away on you... the effect should have worn off by now though, without steady doses."

Cathy thought of the piano, how that song had triggered her memory of the waterfall, and that she had had no idea why. She recalled O'Toole playing the piano in the music room one day, and a similar memory having come to her. She remembered how relaxed she'd become in the car with Xander, practically throwing herself at him, when the piano solo had started. "They were to relax me," she whispered. "To calm me down. But why?"

"Doesn't say," Mike sighed. "I guess we'll never know,

now."

"What else was there?" Xander asked, still just staring forward at the time ticking by.

"Oh, gee..." Mike huffed, running a hand through his hair and wincing as the motion stretched some of his stitches. "He did it to some of the teachers... he'd offer them coffee every day and use that damn handkerchief of his to smear it onto their mugs. Getting them to stay quiet about his techniques and what he was doing with our files, probably."

"Especially Shnieder," Cathy finished.

Mike nodded. "There were other students, too, making sure they repressed memories... like the time the Black Womb attacked Tommy in his bedroom during the whole Tee/Omega thing. He didn't forget it, just never talked about it. Did the same thing to Mandy, made her not talk about what the Tees did to her." He paused, again turning the page, his eyes growing wide.

"What?" Xander said, finally looking over.

"He also programmed certain responses to situations, made her not fight back against the Tees the second time. He made her eat less, made her hormone levels fluctuate, sometimes on an hourly basis... he'd make her period stop suddenly for a month, to make her think she might have been pregnant..."

"She never..." Cathy stammered, he mouth dropping. "...She would have come to me."

"Yeah," Mike agreed, raising a finger. "But he also did that 'think, don't tell' thing to her, too. Made sure she wouldn't say a word."

"What'd he do to me?" Xander asked, turning toward

the wall now.

Mike swallowed. "Made you forget about your first few encounters with the Anti-Womb... probably because he was there, although it doesn't say that outright. Made your bloodlust grow whenever the name Genblade was mentioned, in case you ever needed to defend Circe against him. Made you repress the memories of Sara, Sud... even Julie, unless certain key words activated them... those are all worn off by now, probably months ago."

Xander nodded. "What else?"

His friend sighed, closing the folder. "When you went under the hypnosis, he brought out the Womb. Awoke it in its own trance-like state, triggered memories of killing and maiming inside of it, sated its hunger for blood, all the while merging both of your personas... or at least trying to, seems he didn't get too far with that part."

"Trying to get me in control. Into something they could use," he finished, eyes growing wide.

"So..." Cathy drawled, her mind snapping onto what the boys already had. "You were never getting control, just borrowing it?" she asked, horrified.

Neither responded, just sat there in silence and avoiding eye-contact.

Finally, Cathy looked at Xander, and he at her. Each knew what the other was thinking. That it couldn't end now. Not yet. That all they'd managed to do was go three steps forward... and ten steps back.

"What now?" she said softly, no longer trying to hold back her tears as she pulled her hand away from Xander's.

Neither of them had an answer. They sat in silence.

After a few minutes, Mike's shoulders heaved upward, then relaxed again in a heavy sigh. He spoke three small words that said everything of the situation: "Black Womb lives."

ENGEN TIMELINE

With over twenty novels spread over three different series by many different authors, the Engen Universe of titles is growing every day and into genres we couldn't have imagined! From the original ten book *Coral Beach Casefiles* thriller series, its crime novel sequel series *Xander Drew*, our flagship adventure title *Infinity*, or single-novels like *Jacobi Street* or *light | dark*, there's something in the Engen Universe for everyone with more books by more authors on the way soon!

...But how do the events relate to one another, chronologically? While some astute readers have guessed at the potential timeline (some accurately, some not), we're going to finally set the question of the Engen Timeline to rest.

Turn the page for an up-to-date guide of the ever-widening world of Engen, featuring the works of Ellen Curtis, Ali House, Andrea Hackett, Sarah Thompson, Jay Paulin, and Matthew LeDrew!

In the 10 Years Prior Black September

"Reptilia" by Matthew LeDrew
published in *light | dark*.
Danger descends on a small secluded town in the form of a deadly virus with fantastic and terrible side-effects. Can a small group of doctors escape alive?

Compendium by Ellen Curtis
Three short stories forming the basis for the Engen Universe's ties to suspense, genetic engeneering, and the supernatural. Features the stories "The Tourniquet Revival," "Falling into Fire" and "At Midnight, the Dawn."

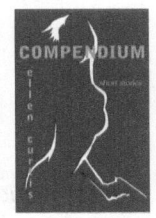

"The Theogony" by Matthew LeDrew
published in *light | dark*.
A tale of young Theo Flaherty of the *Infinity* series and his time admitted against his will to the Black Springs hospital, where he learns to paint, and seeks out his father.

Black September

"Revving Engen" by Matthew LeDrew
published in *light | dark*.
A direct lead-in to both *Infinity* and *Black Womb*, Tasha travels to Coral Beach, Maine on a hot tip about a recently discovered young man with incredible abilities.

Infinity by Ellen Curtis & Matthew LeDrew
Faced with a destiny he's uncertain of, the enigmatic Victor must bring together four unique people with very special abilities... or face the tasks ahead alone. Guaranteed to excite!

Black Womb by Matthew LeDrew
Fifteen years ago, something happened in Coral Beach, Maine that resulted in the present death of a seventeen-year-old boy. Now four high-school students must try to solve the mystery… before the killer picks them off.

Jacobi Street by Matthew LeDrew
When a mysterious painting shows up at an art gallery he works at, Bob must work with Eddie and Sloan to track down its sinister origins and convince the people living on Jacobi Street of them, before its too late!

Transformations in Pain by Matthew LeDrew
When two girls are assaulted and one is hospitalized, the residents of Coral Beach must put their shared tragedies behind them and stop the man responsible, as well as unlock the secrets behind the true nature of the Womb…

Year One: October

Smoke and Mirrors by Matthew LeDrew
The approaching trial of Genblade brings closure to the people of Coral Beach, until people start showing up dead in the same manner they did when he was at large.

"Scarlett" by Andrea Hackett
published in *light | dark*.
Introducing Scarlett, the slightly damaged hunter on a mission to save others from the monsters from her past.

"The Inevitable" by Ali House
published in *The Lightbulb Forest*
A young woman must contend with the
emergence of a frightening new power alongside
the emotional high of a first date.

The Tourniquet Reprisal by Curtis & LeDrew
A man lives in Atlanta, Georgia that people
don't talk about, but everyone knows he's there.
He arrived a year ago and turned a gaggle
of uneducated youth into something new,
something to fear.

Roulette by Matthew LeDrew
As the teen suicide rate in Coral Beach starts to
climb astronomically fast, Xander travels to Los
Angeles to fight his most terrifying adversary
yet… and learns that the only thing worse than
looking for release… is finding it.

Year One: November

Exodus of Angels by Curtis & LeDrew
Victor's enigmatic past is illuminated when
Jaycee accompanies him to visit a new friend
in the paliative care ward of the Black Springs
hospital, where Theo also happens to be
searching for a cure for Leigh.

Ghosts of the Past by Matthew LeDrew
Coral Beach faces its most awesome threat when
one of Engen's past mistakes is unleashed upon
the unsuspecting populous. Friends and enemies
unite to fight a common enemy… but will even
that be enough?

Touch Your Nose by Matthew LeDrew
Simon Monk must infiltrate the San Fransico branch of Shane Industries, a massive company with deep ties to the Engen Universe. Where do his true loyalties lie? And can he get out without causing harm?

Ignorance is Bliss by Matthew LeDrew
After being set through the ringer one too many times, Xander decides that his life with Julie needs a little more attention... which is bad news because a new villain has come to town with his sights set on Adam Genblade.

"Gristle While You Work" by Jay Paulin published in *light|dark*.
A short story centering around the rise of a new, and possibly cannibalistic, serial killer in the Engen Universe.

Becoming by Matthew LeDrew
For months Xander Drew has been doing his level best to keep the streets of Coral Beach clean, which means it's time for the forces of darkness to strike back... all at once.

Inner Child by Matthew LeDrew
Julie is hospitalized with life-threatening wounds to both body and soul. But the real threat comes from the hospital walls themselves, as a demonic presence makes itself known to Xander and his friends.

End of Year One

Gang War by Matthew LeDrew
The Tees, a homicidal gang of evil men, has finally been taken down by Xander Drew. But his victory is short lived, as retired Tees are mysteriously killed. With a town of suspects, anyone can be the culprit… including one of their own.

Chains by Matthew LeDrew
Sociopath Derek Smith has been freed from prison and is praying on the weak; and none are weaker than August Styles: a pregnant girl with Down Syndrome who has run away from home.

"Omega" by Ellen Curtis
published in *light | dark*.
A sinister division of Engen begins a series of experiments on pregnant women in a fashion eerily similar to those that created the original Black Womb project.

The Long Road by Matthew LeDrew
Xander meets the American people — and realizes that the world is harsh and wicked, but can also be soft and gentle, even loving. Xander Drew comes of age on the road, and sets his new direction.

Year Two

Cinders by Matthew LeDrew
Detective Horton enters a violent and dangerous world he didn't know existed beneath the veneer of order and structure that he has based his entire deductive method around.

Sinister Intent by Matthew LeDrew
One of the killers Detective Horton could not catch has resurfaced: a serial killer who flaunts his sinister intent in front of the Los Angeles Police Department, making it so that no one is safe.

Faith by Matthew LeDrew
Xander's mysterious and troublesome past returns to haunt him on the streets of Los Angeles; a place where even more people can get caught in the crossfire of the games of death and deceit that makes up his life.

Flickers in the Night by Matthew LeDrew
Lisa Rowdan is hunted by her haunting -- and powerful -- ex-boyfriend Ryan through a lonely city street. Can she escape him?
One of over twenty great sprine-tingling short stories!

Family Values by Matthew LeDrew
Xander and his new friends Crowley, Lisa, and Tim investigate a series of kidnappings and murders that stretch back decades, all of which have the same similar twist: victims being found after years of being missing.

The Future

Fate's Shadow by Matthew LeDrew
When one of Xander's old cases comes up for trial, Megan Greene returns with it. The former friends are led into conflict regarding her client's innocence. However, they put their difference aside when they both become targets of the vigilante known as Shiro Gilbert.

The Future

"Remers" by Sarah Thompson
published in *light | dark*.
In the not-too-distant future of the Engen
Universe, young athletes are the targets of a
scouting program to create the next stage of super
soldier with cybernetic enhancements.

ABOUT THE AUTHOR

Matthew LeDrew holds an Honours Degree in English from the Memorial University of Newfoundland with a minor in Anthropology, and studied Journalism at College of the North Atlantic in Stephenville, Newfoundland. He was honoured to be a jury member of the 2018 NLBA awards.

He has written twenty novels for Engen Books: the ten book *Coral Beach Casefiles* series, *The Long Road, Cinders, Sinister Intent, Faith, Family Values, Jacobi Street, Touch Your Nose, Infinity, The Tourniquet Reprisal,* and *Exodus of Angels* the latter three of which with co-author Ellen Curtis.

He lives in St. Johns, Newfoundland.